The Monticello Baby Miracles

Double bundles of joy!

Twin sisters, spontaneous Claudia and
reserved Harriet might be chalk and cheese,
but no matter the distance between them
they are each other's best friend.
And then they both get news which
will change their lives for ever!

For the Monticello sisters it seems miracles
will always come in twos…

Read Harriet's story in
One Night, Twin Consequences
by Annie O'Neil

An invitation from the delectable
Dr Matteo Torres to work with orphans
in Argentina is a dream come true for Harriet.
It's also right out of her comfort zone!
And then one night of seduction
leads to a *very* unexpected consequence
and double the trouble!

and

Read Claudia's story in
Twin Surprise for the Single Doc
by Susanne Hampton

Claudia Monticello must accept former
obstetrician Patrick Spencer's help when she
goes into labour in a broken lift! But after
seeing her sons in gorgeous Patrick's arms
Claudia finds herself hoping this handsome
stranger might just be the daddy
her little family needs!

Both available now!

Dear Reader,

Welcome to *One Night, Twin Consequences*. This is the first time I've written a duet with someone—and let me tell you Susanne Hampton is *fabulous* to work with! Kind, thoughtful and, lucky for me, riding exactly the same train of thought. She was the yin to my yang, and I hope you enjoy the intertwined lives and love stories these two sisters share.

I absolutely fell in love with writing about Harriet and Matteo. Matteo because he's totally gorgeous and I'm a sucker for an accent. Harriet because she has about as much grace and elegance as I do—read: very little!

So strap on your seat belts and I hope you enjoy the ride!

Annie O xo

PS Don't be shy. Be sure to get in touch! You can reach me at my website, annieoneilbooks.com, or on Twitter @AnnieONeilBooks.

ONE NIGHT, TWIN CONSEQUENCES

BY
ANNIE O'NEIL

First published in Great Britain 2016
By Mills & Boon, an imprint of HarperCollins*Publishers*
1 London Bridge Street, London, SE1 9GF

Large Print edition 2016

© 2016 Annie O'Neil

ISBN: 978-0-263-26136-3

Our policy is to use papers that are natural, renewable and recyclable products and made from wood grown in sustainable forests. The logging and manufacturing processes conform to the legal environmental regulations of the country of origin.

Printed and bound in Great Britain
by CPI Antony Rowe, Chippenham, Wiltshire

Annie O'Neil spent most of her childhood with her leg draped over the family rocking chair and a book in her hand. Novels, baking and writing too much teenage angst poetry ate up most of her youth. Now Annie splits her time between corralling her husband into helping her with their cows, baking, reading, barrel racing (not really!) and spending some very happy hours at her computer, writing.

Books by Annie O'Neil

Mills & Boon Medical Romance

The Surgeon's Christmas Wish
The Firefighter to Heal Her Heart
Doctor...to Duchess?
One Night...with Her Boss
London's Most Eligible Doctor

Visit the Author Profile page at millsandboon.co.uk for more titles.

I absolutely loved writing this book—
in large part because it was about a big sister…
even if she *is* older only by a minute! Always
competitive, me! Whilst completely different,
Harriet and Claudia share the unbreakable bond
of sisterhood—and for that reason I dedicate
this book with unfathomable love to my sister
Michelle. Xxx

Praise for
Annie O'Neil

'This is a beautifully written story that will pull
you in from page one and keep you up late and
turning the pages.'

—*Goodreads* on
Doctor…to Duchess?

'A poignant and enjoyable romance that held me
spellbound from start to finish. Annie O'Neil
writes with plenty of humour, sensitivity and
heart, and she has penned a compelling tale that
will touch your heart and make you smile as
well as shed a tear or two.'

—*CataRomance* on
The Surgeon's Christmas Wish

'A terrific debut novel, and I am counting down
the days until the release of Annie O'Neil's next
medical romance!'

—*CataRomance* on
The Surgeon's Christmas Wish

CHAPTER ONE

"YOU WANT ME to do *what* tonight?" Harriet all but choked on her freshly dunked ginger biscuit. How did her boss know the perfect way to throw her off balance? Besides, didn't he know nice cup of tea and ginger biscuit o'clock was sacrosanct?

"Give the lecture tonight. You never take enough credit for your work and this would be the perfect way to showcase your research." Dr. Bailey handed her a serviette with a smile. "Crumbs."

"Ack! Oops!"

More mortification. Disintegrated biscuit was now decorating the front of her navy uniform. Typical graceful behavior. Not! Normally the fitted dress flattered Harriet's slim build—created the illusion she was more woman than tomboy. But with a mushy bit of biscuit on her front resembling something more akin to...well... You saw everything in a children's hospital. She accepted the serviette with an embarrassed laugh. She'd had all sorts on her uniform through the years, so this was hardly a disaster. Not that scrubbing her bosom in front of her boss was the epitome of a comfortable moment.

"I don't know…" She opted for the old reliable, "My sister needs me—"

"Your sister lives in Los Angeles. Nice try, Harriet."

"Actually, she's coming over?"

Hmm. That wasn't meant to come out like a question.

"When?" Dr. Bailey was no stranger to Harriet's advanced conversational duck-and-dive technique. This was their drill every time he wanted her behind a podium. Although this time she really did have a legitimate excuse. Maybe.

"She rang last night to say she was coming over." *That much was true.*

"It's a long flight from Los Angeles and in my experience they tend to arrive the next day. Which means you're free to give your lecture tonight."

"Yes, but she's having twins!" Harriet explained, knowing, as the words came out that her very, very pregnant sister hadn't strictly said she was arriving that night and was incredibly unlikely to be appearing until well after the twins were born. A good three months away. Flying weeks before you're due with twins? Not a good idea. Probably not even allowed. Although when her sister set her mind to something, it happened. So that little problem about turning their childhood home into a baby friendly zone over the next few weeks was a nut that needed cracking. Not to mention it being the first time in years her independent sister had well and truly needed her. Enough to add a little kick to her step. Harriet the Reliable was back in action!

Harriet chanced a glance up at Dr. Bailey. Yes. He was still patiently waiting for her to answer.

"You know public speaking isn't really my forte." And that was putting it mildly.

"Since when have you backed away from a challenge?" her boss riposted.

"Since *always* if it involves public speaking!"

"Most people would kill to be the opening act for Dr. Torres."

Harriet kept her lips tightly clenched to hold in

a spontaneous sigh. *Swoon!* Dr. Matteo Torres—the unwitting man of her dreams.

"Harriet…" Dr. Bailey narrowed his eyes. "Has Dr. Torres done something to offend you during his stay here?"

"Uh…no?" Apart from being drop-dead gorgeous, intelligent, a leader in his field and so far out of her league she couldn't see straight. Not that she'd talked to him or anything. Tactical avoidance had been her approach and it had worked just fine during his fortnight of "observation" at St. Nick's. His presence hadn't just made her feel jittery. It made her… Oh, blimey… it made her *lusty.*

Along with ever other red-blooded female in a mile or so's range of the man.

Smokin' hot. Burn the tips of your fingers hot with extra hotness.

And she never said that about anyone. She wasn't trendy enough. By a long shot.

Just catching a glimpse of the man made her feel giddy!

No!

Distracting. Off-putting. Non-essential. Which was why she'd been playing her very own, proactive game of hide-and-*don't*-seek whenever he was within a ward's reach. If she didn't see or speak to Dr. Torres, she wouldn't go all rubber-kneed and act like an idiot. That was her plan anyway and she was sticking with it.

"Matteo is particularly interested in hearing your talk."

"You mean *your* talk." She grabbed hold of the counter edge and feigned a little finger drumming along the worn Formica. *Nope! No rubber knees here!*

"Harriet…there's no need to be modest. It's a chance to shine for our guest!"

"If he's into muttering and stuttering, sure. No problem," she grumbled. Fat chance she'd be able to form a sentence, let alone an entire speech in front of the Latin Lothario, as he was now referenced in the tearoom. Not terribly original, but everyone knew who they were talking about. It wasn't like the corridors of St. Nick's were over-ridden with gorgeous, swarthy obstetricians.

"Harriet." Dr. Bailey put on his stentorian tone. The "dad voice" as she liked to think of it. "This is a chance for you to present your work to the world's largest collection of pediatric elite. People who work with orphaned children all the time. What you've proved here at St. Nick's, and elsewhere, is groundbreaking and could change how wards of the state are treated around the world. Don't you want that for yourself?"

"No!"

Dr. Bailey's expression crumpled to one of pure dismay.

Oops. Wrong answer.

"But I do want it for St. Nick's." A smile lit up her face when an idea hit her. "Hey! What if we have my sister do it by remote video link? She's a gifted speaker and no one would know the difference!"

"Harriet Monticello." Dr. Bailey lost his battle with hiding his exasperation. "You're not an identical twin. What I recall from her odd visit here is that the only thing you two have in common is a surname."

Just because she was a homebody and her sister was exotically thrilling didn't make them all that different!

"Love, you've got this." He gave her arm a reassuring pat. "There is nothing to be intimidated by. I know you prefer being 'the girl behind the screen' but it's time to get you out there. Put yourself in the limelight."

"Dr. Bailey, you're really the public speaker for the department. I'm not sure the Child Care Symposium is really the place—"

"Tush and nonsense!" Her boss cut in. "You're more than capable of delivering the lecture. Apart from which, my wife won't hear of my doing it as it's our anniversary tonight and…I may have accidentally forgotten last year's so you'd be doing me quite a favor. I'm officially in the doghouse until she has a glass of champagne in one hand and a bouquet of roses in the other." His voice shifted back to the confident tone that had won him the trust of countless colleagues and patients. "You're every bit as qualified as I am to give the lecture, Harriet. It was your research that got us the invitation to speak for the CCS in the first place. You should take the credit…" He leaned in for added emphasis. "For once."

Harriet waved away his kind words. "You're the one who gave me the time to do the research."

"And you're the one who connected the dots about the impact of staffing rotas on the children. Take some credit where credit is due! Don't you think it's time to stop hiding behind your sister's shadow?"

"My sister has a very nice shadow, thank you very much," Harriet replied primly, slightly abashed he'd seen through her. Again.

"It's a fascinating topic and many orphanages could benefit. One I know a lot of health professionals will be keen to hear. Including..." Harriet watched the older doctor's eyes scan the ward as if he'd misplaced something. Or, rather, someone.

Their eyes simultaneously lit on the man who'd just set the swinging double doors at the end of the ward in motion as if cued to make a dramatic entrance.

He was tall, ebony-haired and had an easygoing grace about him. Not movie-star-ish. More... cowboy...or fighter pilot. Not a drop of vanity about him. But, sweet cherry pies, did that man ever exude confidence. Hair long enough to see it had a sexy wavy thing going on. Was that a bit of a five o'clock shadow? And...mmm...he didn't just wear clothes, he showed them off. Or did they show him off? Either way, the effect... oh, the effect! Trousers just skimming along his trim hipline. Long legs you could take a zip line ride on if you were into that sort of thing. Shoulders filling out his open-at-the-neck shirt. Not too much. But enough to know that if he lifted a child in his arms there would be some biceps action. Not that she'd imagined him doing that or anything.

Maybe once or twice?

The first time she had seen him—ensuring, of course, she'd been safely tucked behind the curtained confines of a patient's cubicle—her eyes had nearly popped out of her head. Pretty much each time she'd seen him after that? No change.

Raw, unadulterated lust.

There was no other description for it. She had the hots for this man and hiding each time she saw him coming had been her only salvation. Not that she was five or anything. She was just acutely tuned into the child within. It helped with her work. Besides, behaving like a grown-up was highly overrated. Particularly if survival was a factor.

For her entire life, Harriet had been "the sensible twin", the "shy twin", the "wallflower twin" and for about as long as she could remember she'd always happily agreed. Her twin sister, Claudia—

pronounced like a beautiful, fluffy cloud versus a gray, dull clod—was about as vivacious, gorgeous, gutsy and go-get-'em as a girl could get... And Harriet? Polar opposites was a pretty good starting place.

As the doors *phwapped* shut, a surge of energy shot through her so powerfully there was no doubt she would always remember this instant in time. Another daydream to tuck away for the years ahead when Dr. Torres was safely back in his homeland.

The dozen or so patients between them faded into soft focus, their chatter and laughter muted by the thump of her heartbeat ascending to her ears. Everything slowed down, sensations quadrupled and her very breath caught in her throat then released in a sigh as her gaze linked with his incredibly green eyes.

Was that *heat* she felt flickering away below her waist?

Heat?

How inopportune. And... *What were those?* Tingles?

Harriet Monticello didn't get *tingles*, for goodness' sake! And now she was being tickled with *flickering tingles* of *heat*? What was going on?

The closer he got to them, the more she felt everything inside her shift and twist and lift... Good grief!

It wasn't like she was a complete novice in the world of romance. There'd been a handful of boyfriends over the years. Sort of. All of whom she'd parted from amicably. No point in letting them know they hadn't really baked her cake. But responding to a virtual stranger on such a primal level? Brand spanking new.

Was this what *blossoming* was? At a few months shy of thirty, she was a bit late for that, wasn't she? Love at first sight? Or just pure, undiluted desire?

Each microscopic change in her body was wholly in response to him. And utterly involuntary.

He was taller than her, which wasn't difficult— her being the "petite" one to her sister's "statuesque beauty". As he neared, Harriet's chin tipped upwards, opening up the length of her throat in a way that almost felt suggestive. Her shoulder blades shimmied down her back as her shoulders gave a little wiggle to better present themselves. As if such a thing were possible in a staff dress. Sure, it had a clingy cheongsam cut, but it was, at the end of the day, a uniform.

She felt her breasts pressing against the well-worn cotton of the snap-fronted dress, and for the tiniest of moments wondered what it would feel like if Matteo were to trace a finger along the diamond shaped neckline then begin, one by one, to pop open each of the snaps. Would his fingers be rough or smooth? How would it feel if he were to draw one of his hands across her belly and begin to explore elsewhere? Would she touch him back? Or, for the very first time, luxuriate in letting herself be caressed before seeing to her lover's needs? Would his unruly black hair feel as silky as it looked? Would he moan if she scratched his back in an untamed moment of desire? Or call out *mi corazon*! Or whatever hot Latin doctors called out in a moment of passion.

The roar of blood in her ears shot up a few decibels.

When he arrived in front of them—a smile playing across his full lips—a heated flush flashed across her cheeks. Could he read minds as well? Anyone with eyes so lusciously green surely had access to the deeper reaches of a woman's soul.

Er… Get a grip!

Harriet silently tsked at herself. Too many romance novels during the overnight shift. Nevertheless, she did a quick check to see if he really did have thick, dark eyelashes. The final dab of icing on a very tasty-looking cake.

Yup! *Of course he did.*

"Matteo! You found us. I'm so pleased." Dr. Bailey reached out to shake his hand.

She watched as Matteo—*Matteo!*—extended his long, lovely fingers with sun-bleached hairs, not too thick, running along the length of his forearm, and shook hands with her boss. They turned to her, an expectant look in Matteo's eyes, which was when Harriet realized the entire time he'd been walking towards them in slow motion she'd been wiping her disintegrated biscuit into the fabric of her dress right…over…her breast. Classy.

Cheeks properly on fire now, she stuffed her hands into the front patch pockets of her dress, squeezing her eyes tightly shut in a lame attempt to regroup.

"And if I'm not mistaken," she heard Dr. Bailey continue, either oblivious to or trying to cover for her gaffe, "this young woman here is the reason you've come along to see us!"

Harriet's eyes popped open to take an involuntary glance over each of her shoulders. Had one of their colleagues arrived without her knowing? She thought she'd left the rest of the nurses deep in discussion over how to rearrange the supplies cupboard.

Nope. Still just her. All alone with... *Matteo*... and, of course, Dr. Bailey, who was now looking at her with a particularly bemused expression. Maybe she should shut her mouth. Gape-jawed wasn't really her look.

"This is Sister Monticello?"

Oh, sweet wonders of the universe. He had a scrummy accent to boot. Of course he did! The man was Argentinian. What did she expect? Cut-glass British? Even so... It was all sexy and smoky. Yum.

She was pretty sure they didn't make men this—this *male* over here on the sceptered isle.

Or if they did, they were already taken and hidden away by their lucky wives and girlfriends. Too bad she'd all but shelved dreams of having a family of her own… *Stop dreaming!* She adjusted her gaze, eyes narrowing just a bit. Maybe she could dream just a little bit?

Matteo made her want to howl. He probably ate steak. Lots of it, searing it nightly over a naked flame. Without wearing a shirt. Just buckskins and a deep caramel tan illuminated by the flickering fire and a splash of starlight. At which point Matteo turned to her with a smile so warm she hardly knew what to do with herself.

"I was expecting…" Matteo stopped to give a self-effacing laugh. "I am such an idiot. *Sister* Monticello! I've heard so much about you and I'm still not used to calling the nurses 'Sister.' I was expecting a nun!"

"Aha-ha-ha!" Harriet could hear herself giving a weird, cackly, laugh-along laugh. The oh-ho-ho wasn't that funny variety, but if there was anyone in the world who could bewitch the knickers off a nun she would bet her entire sensibly accrued pension Matteo could. Not that her knickers had fallen off or anything. Yet.

He reached out and took her hand, his cheek moving towards hers faster than she could react. As their cheeks met, she inhaled a delicious waft of peppery gingerbread and heard a kissing noise, but didn't feel the touch of his lips. Pity.

"Encantada."

Oh, blimey. Had he just whispered a sweet nothing into her ear?

"It's nice to smell—I mean meet you!" she all but shouted.

What was that? She didn't even know this guy and she was falling to bits right in front of him. Sure, she'd been watching him from afar for the past fortnight. But afar was safe. And right here was….really, really close. He smelled distinctly delicious. So much so, she mused, he really should be a cologne. Eau de Argentine Doc. Man Scent by Matteo. The ad campaign would be a cinch.

Why did her sister have to be eight blinking thousand miles away in Los Angeles just when she'd be *incredibly* handy? Claudia could dig her out of this socially awkward moment without breaking a sweat. Then again, Claudia was drop-dead gorgeous and if she met Matteo before Harriet did, it wouldn't be very good, would it? Even heavily pregnant with twins, her sister was a knockout. She had the pictures to prove it. Harriet felt an unexpected attack of let-him-be mine come over her.

She'd never really cared when the hot man in the room took a shine to her sister in lieu of her. That was how things had always been. But this time…

Calm, calm, calm yourself, Harriet.

It wasn't like she stood even the slightest of chances in the universe of having a man like this one desiring, let alone falling completely and madly in love with her. Like she already virtually was with him. Just a few more minutes and she'd have their china pattern and curtains all picked out.

She ran a hand through her blonde pixie cut, jutting out her lower lip as she did so to blow some air up into the fringe. Another sexy move she'd crafted in how-to-look-like-an-idiot class.

"Nice to meet you, Sister." Matteo held out his hand, which she took and pumped up and down too hard because she was already picturing her cobweb-laced spinsterhood spreading out before her now that she'd ruined any chance of marrying the man of her dreams.

"Harriet's fine—uh…" She made her, *yeesh, I don't know what to call you* face.

"Matteo works—or Dr. Torres if you prefer. I know how formal you Brits are."

"Yes, well…yes."

Was it too soon to dive into the nearest broom cupboard?

"Harriet," Dr. Bailey interjected. "Perhaps you'd like to show Dr. Torres around the hospital? Give him your perspective on how St. Nick's works. He's been trying to track you down for the past fortnight and for some peculiar reason has found it near impossible to find you."

"Excuse me?" Harriet tried her best to wipe the horrified expression off of her face, realizing in an instant she hadn't been successful.

"Seeing that you could be working together in the longer term, it's probably a good idea to get to know each other."

Harriet's jaw dropped again. *Who'd stolen Dr. Bailey and replaced him with this man who was yanking away all her safety blankets?*

Matteo grinned, a glint in his eye betraying

something akin to frustration. "Dr. Bailey didn't tell you?"

"Tell me what?" Her voice was so strangled she was pretty sure the dogs of London would be howling in unison if she continued.

"This trip—my 'visit' here…" He left a small silence to see if she could fill in the air quotes, but there was nothing jostling away the question marks careening round her mind.

Dr. Bailey jumped in. "Harriet, I was going to tell you all about this in good time, but—"

"It looks like—in the hope of some funding— you might be coming to Buenos Aires," Matteo finished for him, an appraising eyebrow arching upwards as he spoke. "To assess me."

His expression shifted into something strangely neutral. It was difficult to tell if he was pleased by the scenario or resentful. Something told her it was the latter. *Great.* Five seconds with Mr. Perfect and already he hated her.

How did one respond to *that*? Her head swung from Dr. Bailey's consternated face to Matteo's unreadable smile. Funding was very dependent on conditions. Lots of i-dotting and t-crossing—

Uh-oh. Wait a minute. She forced her brain to play catch-up.

Was he saying *she* was the condition? She sought each of their faces for answers, feeling a bit like she was watching a tennis match at close range minus the tennis bits.

"Buenos Aires?"

She had been hoping to sound casually interested. Noncommittal. What came out instead was a high-pitched, dog whistle screechy thing. Not really what she'd been going for. Particularly since a trip to Buenos Aires would be about the scariest, most exciting, incredibly interesting, totally top of the list of things she'd never be brave enough to ever consider doing sort of trip. Which was why she had barely ever left the hallowed borders of London town.

"Don't worry." Matteo waved away her response. "I know what it's like to be handed something unwelcome when you least expect it."

"I didn't even know I had been invited anywhere and now I'm unwelcome?" She didn't mean to sound churlish, but c'mon! Every single speck of this was news to her.

"No, no. It wasn't meant like that—but don't

worry. It might not even happen. Nothing's set in stone."

"What if I wanted to see the stone? Part of the stone even?" Harriet pinched her fingers into her best little-bit visual aid. Could you miss something you hadn't even known was going to happen?

Matteo considered Harriet a moment before answering. Apart from looking entirely different from what he'd anticipated, she struck him as a woman who preferred facts over spin. Action over coddling. Someone he could, potentially, work with. Which made a change from most of the research-based medical personnel he came in contact with.

"It's all to do with a possible expansion. More of a new build, actually," Matteo corrected himself. "A clinic. A proper one. And one that's dependent, I am afraid, on charitable donations. Strangely, homes for pregnant teens and orphaned babies aren't big money spinners."

Matteo enjoyed seeing the light enter Harriet's blue eyes at his words. The click of recognition. The spark of interest.

"If they did, I bet Casita Verde Para Niños would rake it in!"

"You know it?" *Impressive.* Most people couldn't name an orphanage in their hometown, let alone one on the other side of the world.

"Of course I know it!" She gave an embarrassed giggle. "Even if I can't pronounce it properly."

All tension dropped from her face and was replaced by utter engagement. Work talk, it seemed, put her at ease. *Interesting.* Maybe the stories floating round St. Nick's were true. All work and no play made Harriet Monticello a delightful woman—because work was her play. The pretty blonde was a far cry from the dried-up nun he'd been picturing.

"Didn't you single-handedly drag children's homes in Argentina into the twenty-first century?"

"Well..." Matteo felt an unfamiliar wash of modesty come over him. "People don't usually see what I do that way." Particularly his socialite parents, whose business dealings saw more money change hands in a single day than he had as annual budget. "Black hole with no economic return" was the more frequently used description. "Of course, you'll know it's quite specialized. It's a place pregnant teens can receive the support they might not be getting at home or are afraid—" He caught himself on the brink of speech-making and held back. "It's nice to hear someone thinks highly of the Casitas."

She gave him a flustered smile and looked away, sidetracking Dr. Bailey with a question about rosters. Matteo examined Harriet again. Given she didn't look a thing like the mental image he'd conjured up, it was little wonder he hadn't singled her out over the past couple of weeks. Particularly given the role her bosses seemed keen for her to play: The Woman Who Would Deign Him Worthy of Funding.

And now she didn't know a thing about it? If the joint clinic meant that little to the board of St. Nicholas Hospital, he may as well turn around and go home. He'd enjoyed the two-week secondment to the high-tech hospital's obstetrics unit, but his main aim was a clinic for his own. Then again… Harriet knew Casita Verde and the work he did without so much as a prompt. *Best not to be too hasty…*

He'd been prepared to go into his usual charm offensive routine. It worked a treat in Argentina's moneyed circles. The elite of Buenos Aires rarely if ever went for earnest, over-keen do-gooders. Appearing as though he could live with or without their money always seemed the best tack. That, and a lavishing of compliments. He had yet to meet an ego that didn't like to be fed. Something told him cocktail-party chatter and superficial compliments wouldn't work with this woman.

She was pretty, in a completely natural way. Gamine, honey-blonde hair, a single swish of mascara on lashes overhanging a doey pair of bright blue eyes. A sweet splash of pink grew on her cheeks when she realized he was looking at her. She seemed…kind. A far cry from the dolled-up heiresses his parents wished he spent more time courting.

"You can't expect your grandfather's trust fund to keep Casita Verde's doors open forever!" they warned on a regular basis—making it more than clear which way their wills wouldn't be bent. Which was fine. He'd done all right so far. And they were family. Definitely not perfect, but they were all the family he had left.

"Great!" Dr. Bailey clapped his hands together and gave them a quick rub as if they'd all just agreed on a ground-breaking deal. "I'll leave you two to it, shall I?"

"No!"

Matteo couldn't help but laugh. It seemed Harriet disliked the position of the "chooser" as much as he hated being the beggar.

"I'm pretty good at being invisible, if you need to get work done." Matteo gave her an out. The last thing a busy nurse needed was a hanger-on weighing her down.

"Sorry, Dr. Torres, I didn't mean you. I just..." The pleading look she sent in Dr. Bailey's direction brought another smile to his face. Harriet Monticello didn't just wear her heart on her sleeve—what she felt was written all over her face. From the looks of things? The idea of spending time with him was pretty low on her list.

Perfect! That made two of them, then. She didn't want someone tagging along after her and he didn't really want a research nurse being posted in the heart of Casita Verde to see whether she deigned him worthy of funding.

But unless teenaged pregnancy became a thing of the past, there would never be a day when the center didn't need more money. Not to mention the fact that money wasn't printed on tears and there would be plenty of those if he didn't get the go-ahead. Their resources were limited, and he was having to toughen his already thick exterior with each girl they were forced to turn away because of a lack of resources.

"Could you tell me just a bit more about this Argentina thing before you disappear off to your candlelit dinner?" Harriet had a hand on her boss's arm now, her blue eyes virtually begging him not to leave.

Dr. Bailey looked like a deer caught in headlights. Matteo leaned against the nurses' counter, trying to look casually interested instead of downright humored. If his own fate hadn't been dangling from the threads of their conversation he would have laughed out loud.

"The board of directors thinks you need some fieldwork. After speaking with Matteo about how things stand at the casitas—the board suggested seeing how you go tonight. How you present yourself."

"So you've known all along I needed to give the speech tonight?" Harriet's eyes opened so wide she almost looked like a child.

"If—*when*—everything goes well…" Her boss stopped to clear his throat and throw an apologetic look Matteo's way. "The board would like you to go out to Buenos Aires for a few weeks—maybe months—to see whether your research could be implemented at Casita Verde. If so, St. Nick's would open a clinical outpost—in cooperation with Matteo, of course. A partnership."

Interesting.

Matteo hid his surprise. She was the one being played. Not him. Unusual.

"You're *bartering* me?"

And it sat with her as well as it sat with him. He was genuinely starting to warm to this woman. Again—unusual.

"One good turn does deserve another, Harriet," Dr. Bailey continued with a patient smile. "You hardly ever leave the hospital, let alone Britain. I thought putting your research into practice in a different—"

"Apologies, Dr. Bailey." Matteo stepped forward, his expression quite sober as he nodded in Harriet's direction. "I probably shouldn't interfere, particularly with the board's decision pending. But I must be clear. Sister Monticello's nursing skills would be valued at Casita Verde, but as far as her research goes? She is welcome to come, to observe and to offer suggestions. Lend a hand where necessary. But changes are down to me. In my experience, academic studies are often just that."

"I beg your pardon?" Harriet's hackles went straight up. "I think you'll find my study comprehensive enough to see the changes we've implemented in *numerous* children's homes here in the UK, including St. Nicks, are making a very, *very* big impact on the children's well-being. My methods *work*." She ground out the word with an imperiously arched eyebrow for emphasis.

Matteo rocked back on his heels and smiled broadly. He liked this woman. She was passionate and about as into playing politics as he was. Not at all.

But if Harriet were to come to Buenos Aires, she would need to toughen up to deal with his "every day". St. Nick's had amenities. Lots of them. He watched as the set of her jaw tightened enough for a muscle twitch. Then again…maybe a stint on his patch would be good for her. And him.

"Shall I leave you two to the ward tour, then? It's Harriet's showcase!" Dr. Bailey had already turned to go, not leaving them much of a choice. Harriet nodded curtly, just the tiniest hint of "don't leave me" left in her eyes as he and Dr. Bailey shook hands.

"Sister?"

Matteo couldn't help grinning as she un-clenched her lips and forced on a "guess we're stuck with each other" smile.

His amusement increased as Harriet excused herself for a moment to fiddle round with some charts in faux preparation for his tour. She obviously wasn't happy about the avalanche of in-formation she'd just been handed. Not to say he was ready to click his heels up in the air in a fit of glee, but none of this was of her making. An unfamiliar urge to make sure Harriet came out of this unscathed niggled away at his conscience. If anything, she was the biggest pawn in the scenario. No point in dumping all of his reservations onto her plate. She tugged her form-fitting uniform down a notch, accenting the perfect swoosh of waist to hip ratio.

Hmm... Perhaps this whole palaver would be easier if she had been a nun.

Nuns? He could deal with nuns. Unlike most of his childhood friends, he'd enjoyed Catholic boarding school—the structure had suited him. A nice contrast to his parent's whirlwind, round-the-globe lifestyle. He'd take a nun over a Buenos Aires socialite any day of the week. Not literally, of course. He shuddered away the thought. Nuns and socialites. Ugh. He stopped another shudder. He'd rather a night of romance with Harriet than—

Uh... *Que paso?* One second he was keeping Harriet at arm's length, the next he...?

No. He didn't. Casita Verde kept him busy. Incredibly busy. Not to mention his "no children" policy that sent most Argentinian women flying out the door. "What kind of man doesn't want children of his own?" they all asked.

One whose sister had died in childbirth. That's who. One who worked with scores of orphans no one wanted to adopt every day. One who'd vowed to be a doctor and nothing more to said orphans, the teens who gave birth to them and anyone else who crossed the threshold into the *casita*. That's who. Not that he had issues. He had facts. And perspective. Children of his own? Not an option.

He looked across at Harriet, still engaged in her chart-juggling. From what he heard, she spent as many hours at St. Nick's as he did at the *casita*. Birds of a feather? He watched her face break into a smile as a sock puppet fell out of one of the record folders.

He doubted it.

She was a wisp of a thing, slight. Complete with flushed cheeks, an untidy swish of honey-blonde hair and clear blue eyes that didn't seem able to lie. *Real.* He liked her. And, coming from him, that was saying a lot. He didn't "do" personal. Couldn't broach "real". Cool, calm reserve. It served him well. And yet...

"Should I go out then come in again?" Matteo offered, pointing to the swing doors.

"Why would you do that?"

"So we could start over. Or—at the very least—it would buy you some time to pretend being forced to have a puppy dog follow you round all day wasn't the worst thing to ever happen."

"Unfortunately, we don't allow dogs in the hospital," Harriet blurted, covering her mouth with both hands in horror after the words flew out.

Matteo laughed and put what was meant to be a reassuring hand on her shoulder. Her shoulders instantly shot up to her ears, briefly trapping his fingers between them. He only just managed to stop himself from running a finger along her jawline as he withdrew his hand, taking a mental note as he did so: Argentine ways were too tactile. This woman needed her space. And he found himself wanting to respect that.

Winning Harriet Monticello's confidence seemed like something of genuine value. He totted up a notch in the pro-Harriet camp and another in the watch-it category to check himself. Being emotional about things—about *people*—didn't get you very far.

"Let's say we get this tour underway."

CHAPTER TWO

"AND NOW FOR one of my favorite places…"

Harriet smiled broadly but widened the gap between them as they made their way to a glass-fronted ward. She definitely liked to keep him at arm's length. He dipped for a surreptitious sniff of his shirt. He was certain he'd showered this morning…

He covered the move with a smile and an earnest nod. "It's nice to see changes implemented that don't necessarily require huge injections of cash.

"The whole world is slashing budgets and we're no different. But it's the staffing changes that make the biggest impact and those are completely free. Makes work seem less like…work."

"It seems to me you do a lot more than work here." And that was putting it mildly. There were staffers and then there were people whose work was their passion—their calling. Harriet knew every patient, staffer, nook and cranny of St. Nick's. Not many people were like that. He felt that way. From the day his sister had died he'd known where to pour his energies. His rage. But Harriet seemed fueled by other fires. She was pure compassion.

"Ta-da!" She twirled around, swirling her hands into a presentation pose as his heart sank. A row of little cots filled with pink and blue bundles spread out before him. The infants' ward. He'd been so busy focusing on Harriet's take on pediatric staffing he hadn't even noticed where they were heading.

"Want to go in for a snuggle? I always come here when I'm feeling a bit down. Baby therapy!" Her eyes sparkled in anticipation of his affirmative answer. 'You know, a whole new world… little tiny fingers, little tiny toes. Endless possibilities!"

Wrong customer. Wrong question. He flicked his eyes towards the large wall clock.

"I think we should probably press on." He knew his smile was tight, but at least he'd managed one of those. "How about we work our way back to your office and I can get out of your hair."

She threw him a questioning look, but didn't press him.

He didn't do cuddling, cooing or coddling. He helped young women through often complicated births, took care of the casita's orphans if they required medical attention—but getting attached to any of them? Not his bag. Caring only led to heartbreak and he'd had more than his fair share of that nonsense.

"Not everyone has the stomach for this kind of work." He tried to cover the awkward silence settling between them. "And yet you choose to be with children most people prefer to ignore. A ward full of dying orphans—"

"Children," she firmly corrected.

"Orphaned children," he couldn't stop himself from riposting. "I'm surprised you, of all people, would wrap everything up in politically correct language to make things softer and fluffier for them. Life is tough and will continue to be so— especially for children like these. Orphans."

From the flash of ire in her eyes it looked like he'd hit a nerve.

"They're *children* first and foremost, Dr. Torres—and that's how I see them. How *we* see them. Not a single one of them is harboring an illusion that the world is solely made up of happy families and that they're on a little spa break, thank you very much. The children in my ward have all most likely come here to die, and they know that. So having things a bit 'fluffy bunny' is *exactly* what we're after."

Harriet only just stopped herself from harrumphing. She prided herself on choosing her language at St. Nick's very carefully and patronizing her about it didn't go down well, no matter how nice a package it came in.

"'Fluffy bunny'?" He arched an eyebrow.

Hmm...that may not have had the gravitas she had been aiming for.

"It's interesting you should ask, *Dr. Torres.* Terminology is one of the things I was going to talk about tonight in my speech. Something that can make a real difference for the *children* here. And very possibly at Casita Verde. I wouldn't like to judge before I set foot in the place."

Ha! Take that, you—you aspersion-caster, you!

"So you *will* be giving the speech tonight, then?"

Another amused eyebrow shifted upwards.

Oh. *Wait a minute.*

"I…" She scanned the ward for an invisible Dr. Bailey. "I think my esteemed boss hasn't really given me much of a choice."

"There is a rather nice carrot dangling at the end of the stick if it goes well, no?"

Her eyes caught his. A ridiculous image of Matteo beckoning to her with a single crooked finger as he lay bare chested on a satin-sheeted bed blinded her for a moment. He wasn't talking about himself, was he?

Was he?

She sought answers in his eyes—almost verdant they were so green. So dreamy green… This wouldn't do. She turned course abruptly in an attempt to swish away down the corridor, only narrowly avoiding tripping over a six-year-old playing airplane. Grace, it seemed, was continuing to elude her.

"Don't you want to show me around your part of St Nicholas's?" Matteo appeared at her side in a couple of long-legged strides. He, apparently, had children dodging down to a fine art.

She didn't answer. There were a whole host of things she'd like to do with him, but show him the place that mattered to her most? Open herself up to more disparaging comments? Not particularly.

"I bet you could have done anything you set your mind to," Matteo pressed, enjoying watching Harriet veer across the corridor to give herself more distance from him. Was she shy, or just repulsed? Not the usual effect he had on a woman, but he was open to firsts. "Were you ever tempted to become a doctor?"

"Ha! Good one. Not for a second. Nursing is exactly where I belong. It suits me perfectly."

Her words sounded positive, but from the expression on her face Matteo could see Harriet's laugh-it-off demeanor was a defense mechanism.

"What's wrong with aiming higher?"

"What's wrong with life in the trenches?" Her expression dared him to come up with an answer.

"Good point." And he meant it. He fixed his gaze to hers—clear and blue, imbued with a healthy dose of trust. Innocent—but not naive. It wouldn't surprise him in the least to discover that what you saw was what you got with Harriet Monticello. What did surprise him was that he wanted to know more. Another first. He switched course.

"Would I be correct in presuming your father was Italian with a surname like Monticello?"

"I thought we weren't going to talk about me." She waved off his question.

"I never said any such thing. You did."

"Was." She nodded, her mood taking a visible dip. "He and my mother—who was Irish…" she pointed at her blonde hair "…died quite a few years back. Gosh…ten years ago. When I was just starting my nursing training here."

"I'm sorry to hear that." And he meant it. Family was precious. He wished he was better at fostering what little relationship he had with his parents. After the fog had cleared in the wake of his sister's death they had all but gone their separate ways. Acknowledging the work he did meant remembering their daughter. He'd already accepted that might never happen.

"It happens to everyone, eventually." Her lips arced into a sad smile as she turned to look out a window towards a flourishing garden courtyard. Not as lush as in Argentina—but it was nice. Another Harriet touch?

He turned and saw her fighting a glaze of tears forming, her blue eyes fastidiously taking a swing round the leafy courtyard. He understood instantly. St. Nick's was filling an emptiness in her. The space her family had filled. The same way his work stood in for what he could never replace. The dreams he would never realize. Would there ever come a day when he'd done enough? A day when he felt at peace?

Something deep within him said no. Something deeper prayed he was wrong.

He pressed his hands onto his thighs before giving them a conclusive clap. This was all getting a bit too deep and heavy and he needed to be on his top game tonight. There weren't just peers in the audience. There were donors. Ones with deep pockets. Including a very pretty research nurse who could be the key to a new clinic.

"Well, I, for one, am looking forward to seeing you ace that speech tonight."

"From your lips—" Harriet began as she turned from the window then stopped, her eyes snagged on Matteo's full mouth. One lip resting atop the other, parting to speak…

"And then you'll come to Buenos Aires and

show me your dazzling research in action?" His smile was leading. He was aware she'd been staring—and that she liked what she saw.

"When you put it that way, how could I resist?" She looked away from his inquisitive gaze. To push boundaries? Change things further afield? Tickles of possibility teased at Harriet's utilitarian shoes and practical hairdo. To live twenty-four seven with a man who turned her into the equivalent of a weeping Beatles fan? Emotional yo-yo? Oh, yeah. She was riding that thing like it was going out of style.

No. No way.

Her sister did wild and wonderful. *She* did sensible and sane. It's why her sister needed her. Why she stayed put, holding onto the family home…just in case. If she wasn't needed, then… *Best not go there.*

"So, I guess I'd better offer you some tips on life in my country," Matteo commented, as if the trip was a done deal. "Lesson number one? In Argentina, there is a lot of kissing. Anything and everything—especially an agreement—comes with a kiss. You'll have to get used to it if—*when*—you come."

He didn't seem like the flirting type, but… Was he *flirting*?

She nodded dumbly.

Wait. Were his lips getting closer? Had her eyelashes just fluttered? She didn't flutter—oh, he was coming closer. Was he aiming for her cheek? Which way was she meant to turn? Right? Left? Was this like the cheek-rub thing earlier with the kissing noise but no contact? Blimey, she wished she'd traveled more.

His hands touched each of her shoulders. Her brain did a little short-circuit before reconnecting with her ability to see straight. Undecided, Harriet changed direction at the precise moment Matteo's very obviously intended cheek kiss landed squarely on her lightly parted lips.

Everything inside her responded to his touch.

Her entire bloodstream surged and performed a ready-for-Vegas dance routine. Had he stayed there…his lips tasting hers…just a little longer than one would for an accidental snog? Or had she made that up? Fact and fiction were blurring at a rate of knots.

She pulled back and instantly wanted more. Matteo was giving his chin a scrub, a curious expression playing across his features. Had she just grown antlers? Insecurity began to unfurl its fingers through her. If this was how things worked in Argentina, she was definitely going to stay right in England where a handshake was a handshake and cheek kisses were precisely what they said on the label.

She tugged her hand from his, took an unnecessary glance at her watch and backed into her office. Keeping her eye on the prey. Enemy? *Something like that.*

"I think I've taken up enough of your time." Matteo stepped back, wondering what the hell had possessed him to give a spontaneous kissing lesson. No one got under his skin and yet...

Harriet gave a nervous laugh and ducked farther into the confines of her office.

No bets on that one. Matteo knew himself enough to know he'd wanted to be close to Harriet, had wanted to touch her. Just a couple of hours wandering around the hospital together and he'd felt a connection he rarely felt. Something genuine. Something real. Not the confident, rule-setting guy who flew to conferences to show his wares in exchange for shiny new clinics.

The Matteo whose heart was every bit as much a part of the *Casitas* as Harriet's was with St. Nick's. The part that was searching for...*enough* and having no idea where to find it.

"I guess I'll see you at the hall?" She shifted from foot to foot, not unlike a skittish colt.

"Yes, perfect." He dug into his jacket pocket and pulled out a wodge of papers he'd folded and refolded into ever-decreasing squares. "I've got all of the details here. What do you call it? The bumph?"

Harriet smiled, a little dimple he hadn't noticed before appearing in her cheek. It made her appear pretty and vulnerable all at once, bringing out a protectiveness in him he hadn't felt for a woman in a long, long time.

"Yes. The bumph. Well done. You're going to have to teach me Argentinian lingo—"

"Spanish? No problem. Dinner afterwards?"

"Uh...I don't know about that."

"Of course you do. Come to dinner with me after the lectures and we can toast your public speaking success."

"I'm not so sure—"

"Sister, can you come?" A nurse knocked and

stuck her head in the door, her face looking strained with worry. "It's Cora."

"Is she seizing?" Harriet scooted round him and was in the corridor in an instant.

"SFS. She says she tastes pickles and has the seasick feeling. She won't move until you come."

Matteo didn't even stop to think. He followed Harriet to the play area the nurse indicated. A simple focal seizure could quickly lead to another much more dramatic attack. Grand mal seizures weren't uncommon.

"Does she usually have a stage two?"

"Yes." Harriet kept up the quick pace. "Childhood absence. Unresponsive to voice, automatisms. Eyelid flickering and some lip smacking," she explained.

"So nothing violent?" Matteo matched her stride for stride.

"No." She shook away her own answer. "She's had one tonic-clonic, but overall she's been responding well to meds."

"Sodium valproate?"

"In combination with lamotrigine. It seems to work well for her. We wanted to steer clear of phenobarbital and phenytoin."

"Adverse affects on cognitive development?"

Harriet nodded. They'd both clearly read the same studies.

Harriet headed towards a skinny little redhead standing in the center of the play area.

"Hey there, Cora." Harriet's tone was soft as she gently lowered herself to the girl's eye level. Matteo nodded approvingly at how Harriet moved—careful not to give the girl any rapid movements to take in. If she was already feeling unwell, too much commotion could make her feel worse. "What do you say we get you to your bed?"

"I don't feel well." Cora's gaze remained static on the wall.

"I know, sweetheart. That's why I'm here. Shall we get you to your bed?"

"I'm too dizzy."

"How about I put my hands on your eyes for a bit and you think of your bed?"

"Mmm-hmm."

Harriet shifted behind Cora. "I'm going to do it now, Cora. All right?"

"Okay." The girl's voice was tiny and frightened. The more stressed she became, the more likely another seizure was.

"Matteo." Harriet's voice was a near whisper. "Could you grab that chair, please?" She nodded towards a well-worn wing chair with high sides and a deep seat.

"Absolutely."

Harriet moved to the side, fingers still covering Cora's eyes, as Matteo brought the chair round—aiming it at a portion of the wall that contained a single horizontal line. When Cora felt well enough to focus her eyes on something, that line could help. Another one of Harriet's touches? He wouldn't be surprised.

"All right, sweetheart. Ready to sit down? We've got Christopher here."

Matteo shot her a questioning look. Christopher?

Harriet nodded at the chair. Apparently it was called Christopher.

His instinct was to laugh but common sense caught up with him as they each took hold of one of Cora's arms and guided her into the chair. The girl was feeling panicked, needed her eyes closed, and required reassurance all at once. If she knew she was going to settle back into Christopher, it would be reassuring. Simple. Clever. He was pretty certain he knew who had thought up the idea and couldn't stop a big 'Aha!" smile from forming as they tucked Cora into the chair along with a couple of throw pillows so she'd feel extra cozy and safe.

A few minutes later, Cora was feeling much better and asked Harriet to take her to her room for a rest.

After she'd been tucked into her bed, they each took a side of the door frame to lean on and watch her for a bit, with Harriet making a few notes in Cora's chart. When she'd finished, Harriet looked across at Matteo, their eyes meeting with a look of mutual understanding. She was much more than an academic. He'd been quick off the mark to slot her into a "books and flowcharts only" file and, while the incident hadn't been an extreme one, she'd shown swift and effective responses to the girl's plight.

He'd need to be a bit more generous in the Doctor Knows Best department. Be open to her input.

A little zip of anticipation surged through him at the idea of Harriet at Casita Verde. There could be more advantages to her visit than he'd thought. A clinic at the *casita*—a proper one—so that they wouldn't have to send the children away to hospital would be a godsend. It near enough gave him physical pain each time they had to sign a child over to the state but their resources were stretched beyond reason. Perhaps with Harriet on their side...

Would she wear that form-hugging nurse's uniform? he wondered. Then stopped himself. Redressing Harriet Monticello was not the route to getting funding. Not the way to stay focused.

He shook his head to clear it as Harriet slipped the chart onto a hook just inside Cora's door. "I'm off to see a couple more of the kids. Did you want to come?"

It didn't sound like an invitation and he needed to get his head straight.

"I think I'll leave you to it. Make sure I'm at my best tonight." He was about to give her a wink and a smile, but thought better of it. He was no Casanova, and this was a business trip...

He cleared his throat a bit too pointedly. *¡Qué quilombo!* Wasn't he the one who liked keeping things professional?

He tipped his head towards Cora's room as they walked away. "Has she been here long? She seems to rely on you."

"Only a couple of months. She'd been in foster-care, but the parents… The parents weren't up to it." Her lips tightened before she quickly shook off any judgment she'd been going to make.

More kudos to her. He was judgmental as hell when it came to backing out on a commitment like that. Better not to make one at all. That's what he did. The only commitments he made were professional. It made life much easier.

Harriet pointed to a large, colorful chart with names and times on it. "The children know the shifts and have one person of their choice to call on when they're feeling anxious. She hasn't chosen yet, so I'm the interim 'go to' girl."

"Is this part of your staffing thing?" *How about sounding a bit more patronizing?* He could've kicked himself.

"It's part of being consistent with the children. Something, as you well know, most of these kids haven't had." She swept away a lock of blonde hair before continuing. "Cora, like a lot of the residents here, had been in a foster home. Well, several foster homes, and she also has minor ADHD that kicks up a notch with each change. The more anxious it makes her, the worse her epilepsy becomes, and the worse her epilepsy becomes—"

"The harder it is to place her," Matteo finished for her. It was the same drill where he came from. The worse the medical condition, the less likely it was they'd find adoptive parents, let alone foster parents. Who wanted to open their wallets, let alone their hearts, to a child with so many hurdles to leap?

"Got it in one!" She smiled up at him, another one of those hits of connection pinging him straight in the chest. Practical, emotional and as committed as they got. This woman was a medical triple threat.

"It looks like we might have more in common than I thought." Matteo gave her a rueful smile. "Professionally speaking, of course."

Her smiled disappeared in an instant.

Why had he said that?

He knew exactly why he'd said it. To keep his emotions where he liked them. All tucked up in his very own…er… Christopher. But taking away that smile of hers? A bad move.

"Of course. Well, then…" Harriet's voice became clipped. "If you don't mind, I'd like to finish seeing the pa—the *children* and then get home to work on my lecture. I don't want to be letting you down tonight. Professionally speaking, of course."

Touché.

CHAPTER THREE

"YOU STOOD ME UP."

Harriet screamed and flew out of her office chair at the sound of Matteo's voice.

"What are you doing here?"

"Trying to find my dinner date."

"What?"

"You said you'd have dinner with me."

"But that was…" *Before I made such a hash of things.*

"That was what you agreed to do after the speeches. So…" He looked around what he could see of the ward from Harriet's doorway. Low lights, a couple of nurses huddled at a station farther down the corridor, some classical music coming from one of the children's rooms…exactly the type of mellow atmosphere she'd needed after Speech-gate. Being at St. Nick's always centered her.

Well, it had always centered her before a certain Argentinian doctor had started creeping round corners, insisting on people going out to dinner with him.

"C'mon. Your shift ended hours ago. Get your coat."

See? There was no telling the man.

"I'm not really hungry."

That should shush him.

"Keep me company, then?"

Um... Waver, waver, waver.

His voice was gentle. It was obvious he was trying to make her feel better and she was grateful to him for that. She tangled a couple of fingers into a loose twirl of hair just to up her maturity factor a notch.

"It's my last night in London. You can show me the sights!"

Harriet laughed. "I think I'd be about the worst tour guide ever."

"Why? This is your home, isn't it?" He spread his arms wide as if to encompass the whole of London.

"This is my home is more like it." Harriet indicated the ward.

"Well, then, you're all dressed up. It would be

a shame not to go out and explore together—at least a little."

Harriet shot him a noncommittal look. She didn't *do* spontaneous! Didn't he get that? Then again… Another image of herself draped in cobwebs, an aged version of her "public speaking dress" layered with dust flitted past her mind's eye. Not particularly appealing…

"C'mon. I have a few more hours left. Shall we explore together?" He jigged his shoulders up and down in anticipation, then held out a hand. A lovely hand. All five fingers gave a little open-close gesture indicating she should take it. Her temperature went up a degree. Or seven.

He looked so…sweet! Like a young man arriving to pick up his first date. A few nerves, a bit of bravura.

He had come back *all this way* to find her. How had he known to—? Okay. Okay. She was predictable and it had taken him less than a day to work it out.

She felt a grin forming. It was the first time she'd seen him look…not vulnerable… Equal? On the same level. That was it. Two colleagues. One night. And a handful of hours.

She didn't do spontaneous. She didn't do flirty. But Matteo was flying back to Argentina before she began her next shift. What could go wrong in just a few hours? Or…what could go right?

She pressed her nails into her palm as if it would give her more courage.

Claudia would say yes. She would've already been out the door.

"Why not?" Harriet grabbed her discarded pashmina from the back of her chair and twirled it round her shoulders à la Claudia. If her sister was brave enough to have twins on her own then she could surely manage having dinner with a man she'd never see again. It wasn't like she'd make a complete idiot out of herself. She'd already cracked that nut at the lecture hall.

She looked at her hand in his, felt a shiver of anticipation run up her arm then made herself give him a smile. *In for a penny…*

"Well, thanks for showing me what I won't be having."

Harriet tried to tack a fun, spirited laugh onto the end of her last bite of Argentinian steak but Matteo could see the words were forced.

"It's just a glimpse." He pointed his knife at the nearly empty plate. "This is passable. Not as good as at home but passable." Matteo took a final bite of his steak, speckled with the piquant chimichurri sauce. "But the *asado*?" He made a *mmm... yummy* sound and licked his lips. "The *asado* is to die for. You can come here and have *asado*. I give you permission to think it is just like home." He smiled, then clarified. "My home."

Harriet stared at him, her forehead crinkling in a growing picture of dismay.

"I can't believe I was so awful tonight!" She groaned, pushing her plate away and letting her head collapse into her hands. When she peeked through her fingers at Matteo she looked so adorable he had to resist reaching across and ruffling his fingers through her hair. And not in an aren't-you-a-cute-kid kind of way. She'd lost her nervy edge over the hours, replaced by excitement at their shared passion for the work they did. He could've talked to her all night long. He hadn't met someone who had kindled that sort of response in him in... *Dios*, was it *ever*? He felt something grow within him he hadn't felt in a while.

Regret.

Regret that he wouldn't have more time with her. There were so many dimensions to Harriet Monticello he had yet to discover and yet part of him felt he knew her already. A kindred spirit. He would've genuinely enjoyed taking his time getting to know her.

He leaned back in the booth seat and drummed his fingertips along the table's edge. "Maybe it's not all terrible. Look on the bright side. At least you got your message through to the person who counts most."

She raised her blue eyes a fraction above her fingers. "Yeah, that'd be about right. And who exactly do you think I impressed?"

"Me!" He reached across and stole a forkful of leftover chimichurri sauce. "Don't look at me like that! How often do you think I sit through four-hour dinners with uninteresting people? Particularly when I have a flight in…" he glanced at his watch "…about six hours from now."

"Uh…not very often?"

"*Sí, correcto.* In fact, I think it'd be a safe bet to say never." He looked her square in the eye.

"Life's too short. Too precious to waste time not doing what you believe in."

Their eyes met for a moment and he felt a genuine hit of attraction for her. Not just the superficial one he'd enjoyed when they'd first met but a genuine tug of desire hitting him in the solar plexus. He looked away.

"I believe in what I said," Harriet answered miserably. "I just couldn't communicate it effectively."

"You've been pretty coherent the last few hours." He pressed his back into the booth seat and shifted his position. *Mind over matter.*

"That's different." She shook her head as if trying to get the facts straight.

"Why? Because you think you could show me a thing or two?"

"Yes." Her eyes popped wide open. "I mean no! Oh, blimey. Do you see what I mean? If there's a chance to stick my foot straight in it, I do it."

"Stick your foot in what?"

"It," Harriet answered. Then giggled. "Language barrier! Oh…let's see."

"Harriet." Matteo's voice went down a notch, latching onto droll. The English weren't the only ones with a dry sense of humor. "I knew what you were talking about, I was just trying to see if you knew why you found addressing a crowd so difficult."

"Oh. Right." Her lips twitched, her eyes solidly on the plate.

"*Cara*, you've missed my meaning. I think what you have to say is wonderful. I'd be lucky to have you come to Casita Verde, even if..."

"Even if what? I tanked it in front of the people who were going to let me go?"

"You would've come if they'd said yes?"

She drew a smiley face in the remains of her sauce before the weary waiter scooped up their plates. He grinned at her and she smiled back, apologizing for keeping him so late. That was who Harriet was. A woman who did countless little kindnesses, expecting nothing in return.

"I would like to think I would have. If I would've been of any use," she added quickly, popping her finger into her mouth where he could just see her tongue circling away, retrieving the remains of the sauce.

He shifted in his seat again and cleared his

throat. Staying...*neutral* was becoming more difficult.

"I'm fairly certain you would have been nothing but an asset." And he meant it.

"Well, that's just grand, then, isn't it?" She gave him a sad smile before trying to scrub away the frustration. "Too bad the board is no doubt busily shredding my name into oblivion and looking for another suitable candidate." Harriet dropped her hands from her face and began to twist her serviette this way and that. "Hey! Maybe we could form a mutual admiration society across the seas!" She shimmied her serviette across the table to him, having folded it into the shape of a little swan, and grinned.

"It's a shame." Matteo picked up the bird and admired her handiwork. He was actually going to miss her, this woman he hardly knew. "I would've liked to work with you."

"Me, too." She raised her gaze from the table and met his eyes. "But I guess some people just aren't meant to stray from their path."

"What do you mean by that?"

"Oh, nothing really. It's just..." she reached across the table and took back the swan, untwisting it as she spoke "…sticking to what I know has always been a good idea."

She smiled up at him, something clouding the azure clarity of her eyes. Disappointment? Sorrow?

"And what would happen, exactly, if you did something new?" He bridled on her behalf. "Are you going to sit there and just let them decide your future for you?" As the words came out, he was surprised to hear the heat behind them. He actually wanted her to come to Casita Verde. See what he'd done. Offer a new perspective. Just a few hours with Harriet wasn't near enough. He wanted more.

"That's more my sister's terrain!" Harriet tried to laugh away his suggestion. "She's the real star in the family," she finished quietly. It sounded practiced. Something she was far too used to saying.

"And is that something you tell yourself or something someone else is telling you? If they are, they need their eyes and minds tested," Matteo protested.

"I'm not sure I follow."

"Well, let's see." He held up a finger for each

point. "You're beautiful. Intelligent. You've turned the lives of countless children into something they can bear. Your sister must be pretty amazing to overshadow all that."

"She is," Harriet replied without hesitation, their eyes locking as she spoke. "She really is."

There was no jealousy in her words, just admiration. The same way he'd felt about his sister. Just love. No expectations.

"I'm getting hot." Harriet started fanning herself with the hem of her pashmina, her eyes suddenly keen to alight anywhere but on him. "Are you hot? I think maybe I could do with a walk."

Harriet shot out of her chair without a second glance at Matteo. Their conversation was getting a bit overwhelming. Out on the street she gulped in a lungful of cool air as if she'd been suffocating.

Maybe she had been. Not from Matteo. Not by a long shot. But from the things he was saying. The cages he was unwittingly rattling? He was rapidly unzipping the safe, cozy cocoon she'd built for herself and had been terribly happy in, thank you very much. Her sister needed her to be the stable one, the one who didn't change. That was her role. Wasn't it?

Then again…what exactly would happen if she took some chances of her own?

She blew out a slow breath, trying to regain some perspective. But all she could see was herself through Matteo's eyes: a woman too frightened to change.

"Harriet! *Chuchera!*" Matteo ran to catch up with her. "Are you all right?"

"Yes, fine." *No. Not even remotely.*

"Sorry, I was just paying the bill, and then you were—" He stopped, his hands taking ahold of her shoulders and turning her towards him. "Are you all right, *chuchera*?"

Harriet nodded dumbly. He was…divine. Exactly the type of man she'd never imagined being with and now he was hunting her down after failed speeches, paying supper bills she'd scarpered on and running after her to make sure she was all right?

One ticket for Matteo the Dreamboat Ride, please!

Her eyes widened. Not exactly a hostess with the mostest moment.

"You shouldn't have paid the bill!" She started digging in her handbag for her purse and felt his hand slip down her shoulder to her wrist, stopping her frantic movements. If there was such a thing as sexy lava it was pouring through her everywhere Matteo's fingers had touched and doing a swirly, pooling thing in her belly. She didn't dare look at him. She was superimposing far too much on him. It was easy to make someone into perfection when you only had eight hours together. Eight amazing hours. The knowledge that they would quickly come to an end all but brought a cry of despair to her throat. She curled her lips in past her teeth, dragging them back out, no doubt pale with the absence of blood in them. Feeling the sting of pain at what she'd never have.

"How do you fancy a walk along the river?" She used her best tour-guide voice. "It's really lovely at night. I'm sure you'll just love the Houses of Parliament!"

It wasn't much of a surprise to Matteo that their riverside walk was both bereft of conversation and came to an end at St. Nick's. Something had passed between them after dinner and Harriet hadn't looked him in the eye once since then.

He watched, smiling, as she peeked into each of the children's rooms, pulling up a bit of duvet here or there, tucking in a wayward teddy bear or two. It was obvious to see the place was Harriet's go-to comfort zone.

He couldn't really judge. He actually *lived* at the original Casita Verde. The fact that it had been a monastery in its former life appealed to him. Solidified his future. Not that his life was entirely monk-like...he saw women. Occasionally. Women who wanted nothing more than a fling—because he never promised more. The likelihood of a woman agreeing to live at Casita Verde and never have children of her own? Pretty slim. So monk's quarters suited him just fine.

"Now we have to be very, very quiet." Harriet held a slim finger to her lips as they made their way across the open common area. "This bit of flooring is super-creaky and I promised the other nurses I wouldn't come back."

"Why?" Matteo grinned down at her, all hunched shoulders and poised on tiptoe. "Are you the big bad boss?"

"The research nurse with no life is more like it." Harriet's mouth shot into an apologetic *oops* position. A perfect red moue.

This time he laid a finger on her lips. She had a life, she just didn't have confidence, and Harriet was a woman who should have confidence in herself.

In the instant their eyes met the atmosphere went taut with something he knew he didn't want to fight again. Something that had been fizzing and crackling away between them from the moment they'd met.

Beneath the pad of his finger he felt the accelerated rhythm of her pulse beating in sync with her heart. Her pupils were dilated in the dim light of the corridor, nearly eclipsing the luminous blue irises. Her breath was held so tightly in her chest he could feel the release against his own when she let finally let herself breathe again. She blinked a couple of times, lips still pressed to his finger. It took him a moment to appreciate she hadn't pulled back. She was responding to his touch.

Before he could stop himself he was kissing her with an urgency he hadn't thought himself capable of. His hands slid up and along her back, straight up the center of her spine, enjoying the feeling of her body responding to the movement of his hands as he did so. Holding her slender frame against his own felt entirely natural. And unbelievably satisfying.

He was surprised at the surge of desire eclipsing his ever-present pragmatism. After tonight, the chances they'd see each other again were slim to nil. More likely nil. But meeting Harriet, he was shocked to realize, had meant something to him. The fact he'd come to find her to see if she was all right after the speech, insisting they go to dinner, talking and walking for hours were absolutely out of the ordinary. He didn't hunt down complications. He never sought love. And now here he was, kissing her as if his life depended on it.

"We shouldn't be doing this."

Harriet's lips moved against his as he teased kiss after kiss out of her.

"Why not?"

"The children?"

"Are you asking me or telling me?" Matteo murmured as his thumb gently pressed and moved along her jawline, exposing the creamy expanse of neck he was itching to kiss and explore with his tongue.

A low gasp of pleasure vibrated along Harriet's throat as he nibbled and tasted his way towards the nook between her neck and the extra-sensitive spot just below her earlobe. When his teeth gave her earlobe a little tug, the resonance of her response deepened to a groan of unmistakable pleasure.

"Let's go to your office."

He felt her entire body tense then, as she made a swift decision, turn electric with intent.

It was all Harriet could do to stop herself from jumping up, wrapping her legs round Matteo's sexy waist and begging him to take her right there and then. She settled for exercising the most self-control she'd ever had to use for the thirty-second race-walk to her office.

This was a carpe diem moment if ever there was one. The chances of a man like Matteo igniting her intellect and her body coming around again? Non-existent to…ooooh, never again in her lifetime! Especially with months—years—of diapers, laundry, feedings and who knew what else that would consume her time once her sister arrived with the twins. She'd be back to being Harriet the Reliable. Tonight she wanted to be Harriet the Wild One. Harriet the Brave.

Kissing and touching and being held by a man who had made her believe in herself for a few ridiculously perfect hours? It was an emotional risk she was going to take.

Just once.

She owed herself that. To see what it felt like to *live*.

The door to her office had barely clicked shut before Matteo had her pressed up against the wall, the fingers of one hand teasing along the décolletage of her wraparound dress. Her breasts were instinctively pressing up against the suggestion of a touch, practically begging him to caress them as his other hand held both of hers above her head in a surprisingly sexy clinch. Fully clothed, aching for more and wholly aware of the growing urgency of desire between them had her feeling saucy and emboldened.

She had never, not once, ever, in her deeply practical life had naughty sex. And right now it was all she wanted. If there had been a pair of pink feathery cuffs in her desk drawer she would be pleading with him to use them. She wished she'd worn her sexy-girl boots her sister had given her, but she'd never felt scrumptious enough to dare. Until now. Matteo was bringing her body alive in a way she hadn't dreamed possible.

"Are you sure you want to do this?" She was surprised at the husky sound of her voice. *Where had that come from?*

"Shouldn't I be asking you that?" Matteo replied smoothly with a tropically heated wink.

How did he even do that?

The look that passed between them as he lazily traced a finger across her collarbones said they both knew what was happening here. They were two consenting adults who would never see each other again. After tonight they could go back to being strangers who occasionally saw one another's names in medical journals.

Would it have been amazing to go to Argentina and dazzle him with her research? Absolutely. Would she trade that for the kisses and touches bringing her body to heightened levels of response? Not that she really had a choice in the matter, but, *Oh, yes*! Again and again and again.

Unexpectedly, Matteo's hand slipped beneath the fabric of her dress and cupped her breast. Harriet had to stop herself from crying out as he swept the fabric aside, unclipped the front clasp of her bra and took her breast in his mouth. Her nails dug into his hand, still holding hers tight against the wall. The last thing she felt like was a captor. She wanted to be taken. She wanted to be his.

Her breath quickened as his tongue took its lazy time exploring first one breast, then the other, her nipples instantly peaking at each touch of his tongue. If her hands had been freed she would have dragged him up to receive countless hungry, insatiable kisses. Held against the wall, she understood, for the first time, the luxury of only being able to respond, reveling in the generosity of the layers of pleasure he was unwrapping within her.

Matteo's free hand shifted away the fabric belt and then the skirt section of her dress, his fingers moving along her stomach, her hipbone, her— *Oh!* His mouth covered hers the instant her cry of response became a moan of sheer, undiluted longing. His fingers slipped and slid, explored and discovered, as her brain short-circuited with need. All her body could do was respond to his touch. She flicked off her heels and went on tip-toe as her legs parted to receive the strokes and cupping of his hand, the shift of fingers, until she couldn't bear it any longer and was forced to give in to heated wave after wave of release.

"Please," she whispered. "I want you."

"Are you sure you want to do this?"

A twist of panic caught up with her longing. Protection. Her nurse's brain kicked into turbo gear. She'd given a few classes on safe sex to the older residents. Did she have anything in her office? She definitely didn't in her handbag. Had never even *presumed* to have something in her handbag.

"I'm not sure I have protection."

"We have to use something." Matteo's voice was thick with emotion. "Practice what we preach."

"Of course. Absolutely!" A nervous giggle leapt past her lips. "The voice of reason speaks!" She was grateful to see a smile playing upon his lips as well. Wouldn't that be rich? A nurse working with orphans getting pregnant from unprotected sex with a man she would most likely never see again. The tabloids would love a naughty nurse scandal. For about thirty seconds. And then she'd have to deal with everything on her own. Just like her sister—

Stop!

She had to stop thinking. Thinking too much was what had made her The Sensible One. The one who didn't take risks.

Tonight? She wanted to be the one who finally, at long last, came out of her cocoon. *Sensibility be damned!*

At least for tonight.

She wiggled out of his hold, her dress shifting along her sides, the cool evening air sending a tickle of goose pimples across her belly. Unbelievably she didn't feel like a class-A idiot.

She felt sexy.

All barefoot and tiptoeing across her office to scrabble in the back reaches of her desk for a condom? This was better than a soap opera! She pulled the wide, central desk drawer open. The one with the dull-from-use pencils, the pen caps without an owner, the mishmash of medical brochures she'd not read yet, or might not ever have a chance to read.

As she stretched and reached into the farther reaches of the drawer she felt Matteo's hands glide over her hips and across her buttocks. Her body swayed along with the exploratory cadence his hands made along her body, bringing out a great desire *to find the blinkin' protection* as soon as humanly possible. Urgency overtook the need to be tidy. Office supplies were flying out of her hands any which way. *Where were the condoms?*

The more intimately Matteo's hands explored, the faster she expelled items from the drawer until, after what felt like forever, she felt a foil-lined packet with a familiar shape. She grabbed it triumphantly and turned around, holding it between them like a trophy.

Matteo tugged his fingers through the twisted tendrils of her hair, the pins plinking to the floor as he pressed himself against Harriet's body. The red-blooded Latin side of him surged to the fore. He wouldn't be able to leave without having her. Feeling her skin against his as she responded to his caresses forced a decision.

"Me quiero que seas mío." His voice was gruff with desire. He wanted her and he wanted her to know how much.

Harriet pressed herself against his erection, her teeth taking hold of one of the buttons of his shirt in an untethered, primal attempt to get closer. He almost laughed at the wonderfulness of it. Had he seen the tigress in her when they'd first met? The kitten maybe. Now she was ready to roar.

He ripped his shirt up and over his head. Another two seconds and Matteo had dispensed with both of their sets of clothes. He turned Harriet round to face the wall, hands shifting along the shivers that accompanied his touch. He was moved by her response to him. Again it struck him how real, how true a person she was. Harriet could only be herself. A part of him regretted that they would never know each other beyond this night. The thought doubled the intensity of his desire. He wanted to know he could tap the part of his mind busy memorizing the feel of her skin, her scent, her gasps and soft cries of pleasure at his touch. He'd take his time, give them each plenty to remember.

Restraint was harder to exercise in practice.

The tigress was well and truly alive in Harriet. Having already brought her to one peak of desire, Matteo was soon clear she had more than enough energy to burn. As he pressed against her, luxuriously enjoying the sensation of her bum shifting and wiggling against his erection, she trapped two of his fingers in her mouth and began to suck them in an achingly slow foreshadowing of what he would be feeling when he was finally inside her.

Wicked thoughts of Harriet in a nun's habit flashed past his mind's eye, sending long pulses of heat straight through to his very marrow. If she'd been all prim-and-proper nursey this morning, she was anything but tonight.

He whipped her round to face him, cupped her buttocks and pulled her up until her legs encircled his waist. When he went to kiss her, he saw she held the wrapped condom between her teeth, eyes glinting with anticipation. One swift move and he cleared her desk of the debris she'd covered it in. Being tidy was the last thing on his mind.

From the luxuriously slow cadence with which Harriet was unwrapping the packet, Matteo could see she was savoring each moment they had together. Yes, it was to be a one-off—but, by God, it would be memorable.

She touched and tasted the length of his erection, before beginning the excruciatingly sexy act of sheathing him. He marveled that he'd ever thought her shy at all. Now wearing only a single strand of necklace gently weighted with a tiny locket, Harriet Monticello was a first-class seductress.

Unable to hold back any longer, Matteo lifted her in his arms, slowly lowering her until they were together, exchanging heat, sharing a heartbeat. He backed her against the wall, moving slowly at first then swiftly, deeply, until his only option was to join her in an intense, full-bodied release. He felt her teeth dig into his shoulder, her breasts pressed into his chest as he came inside her again and again. When their breathing had steadied, he stayed inside her, unwilling to break the spell. Once they said goodbye, he would never see her again.

Just thinking it hurt. Going through it would hurt more. But he didn't do relationships. And he didn't do love. All it led to was heartbreak.

Work. It was the only way he was ever going to

heal the hole his sister's death had left in his soul. The only way he could try to make things right.

He tipped his head back, enjoying the sensation of Harriet's fingers tracing the muscles of his back, his sides. She asked for nothing. She seemed to be completely at one with the intimacy they had just shared and he found himself fighting the feeling of completion it elicited in his heart.

How could he do it? Expose himself to the pain loving someone inevitably brought? He tugged her a bit more tightly into his chest and enjoyed her body's response. A little shimmy and nestling into the angle of his neck and shoulder as he lowered them both to the floor, her legs still wrapped tightly round his waist as if she would never let him go. Perhaps she was coming to terms with saying goodbye as well.

He closed his eyes and breathed Harriet in, painfully aware he was in danger of losing the battle of wills with himself. If anyone was able to handle the extremes of his life, he believed it would be Harriet. The incredible highs. The lows haunting him to this day.

Would she understand that was who he was?

Both light and shade? Someone very likely in need of a good woman to help ground him? Someone at risk of drowning in his own vain efforts to make his sister's death be of some value? Someone who would never bring another child into this world?

No. She deserved more. She deserved everything her heart desired and, blinkered as he was, he couldn't see a way to give her a world of happiness.

"Amorcito." Matteo gently unlocked her feet, still twisted at the base of his spine, and slowly began the inevitable separation, finishing with a soft kiss on her forehead so he could avoid the questions in her eyes. "I must go."

CHAPTER FOUR

"HARRIET!"

Thunk.

"Oops! Are you all right there? I didn't mean to make you bang your head."

Harriet reversed out from beneath her desk. Funny the things that had turned up there this morning.

"Are you all right?"

Dr. Bailey's voice was a bit too bright for first thing in the morning. She looked up at him and attempted a smile.

"You're looking well!"

Check that. *Far* too bright.

Harriet wasn't nursing a hangover—she'd steered clear of drowning her sorrows. What she was nursing? Something much more debilitating. A what? A sex-over? It wasn't like she was used to having wanton sex in her office. Or, more accurately, it wasn't like she was used to having wanton sex, full stop.

Or was everything she was feeling post Matteo's abrupt departure a twenty-four-hour version of a broken heart? When he'd left, it had felt as if her personal wattage had been lowered to dim. She hadn't even bothered going home. A sneaky shower in the surgical ward, a pair of scrubs and one of the sofas had seen her through until dawn. Opening her eyes to a new day hadn't been the rose-colored wonder she'd been banking on.

It had felt, for the first time since her sister had left years ago, lonely.

She had been missing something. No, that wasn't it. She'd been missing *someone*.

She looked beyond Dr. Bailey's feet, a bit surprised to see the stapler had been flung to the opposite side of her office—but at this stage in the game anything could have been anywhere. Last night had been... Last night had been just about the most scrumptious, unreal thing she thought she'd ever lived through.

"Bit late for a spring clean, isn't it, Harriet?"

"What? Sorry?" Harriet scrambled up from the floor, her mind shifting into work mode after a decidedly X-rated journey elsewhere. "Sorry, Dr. Bailey?"

"I said it's a bit late for a spring clean."

She looked at him blankly.

"It being July and all."

"Ah. Yes!" She put on her bright, efficient voice, realizing her office was still looking a bit more post-cyclone than uber-organized. Her normal mode. As if she had a normal any more now that she'd had such a wickedly wonderful night with… *Matteo.* She couldn't even think his name without her belly launching into a heated pole dance.

"Well, it's a good thing you're setting your office to rights as your replacement will be needing everything clearly laid out."

If eyes could actually boing out of their sockets Harriet was certain hers would've chosen this moment to do so. Was she being fired?

"I beg your pardon?" *There weren't cameras in the offices, were there?*

"You'll be off soon."

"Off?" She felt as dumb as she was certain she sounded. A spinster and jobless? She should've stayed under the desk.

"Yes. To Buenos Aires."

Her breath caught in her throat. *Wow. Tongues really did go dry when shocking news was received.*

"Do you fancy a cup of tea?" she croaked.

"Don't you mean yerba mate?" Dr. Bailey chortled. "You'll be wanting to hone your Spanish skills, my dear." Dr. Bailey gave her a warm smile before nodding towards her wall calendar. "The board would like you to head out to Buenos Aires to work at Casita Verde in a fortnight or so—at end of the month at the latest. Time enough for a handover and a quick Spanish course."

"But I was terrible!"

"Well…" Dr. Bailey coughed away some embarrassment. "I did hear things might have gone a bit better. But we received an email this morning from Dr. Torres saying the two of you had had an in-depth talk afterwards and his impressions were all very favorable."

Too right!

Harriet made a nondescript noise, hoping it said, *Yes—we spoke academically all night long.*

Nothing naked happened here. No nakedness at all.

"It's your work, not your public speaking the board is really interested in. So—if you're up for a risk, a bit of excitement, you're heading to new climes."

"Great!" she said in her fake happy voice, taking a slurp of day-old tea that had survived the night's cyclonic lovemaking.

"You did get along with Dr. Torres, didn't you, Harriet?"

"I'm sorry?" Harriet all but spat out her tea before realizing he'd not said "get it on." *Ooh, subconscious! Quit your trickery!*

"So you wouldn't mind working with him?"

It was, of course, in that moment that Harriet eagle-eyed one of Matteo's socks, which was hanging from the filing-cabinet drawer. She sidled over to block it and put on her best casually delighted face.

"No! Absolutely not. Fine. Just fine."

"Well, that's just fantastic! I was hoping you'd be pleased. The two of you have so much in common."

Like the smokin' hot passion we gave in to all

because we thought we'd never see each other ever again!

"Now, Harriet. Don't look so worried. We'll look after everyone and everything here as if you were doing it yourself."

Harriet was feeling the foundations of who she believed herself to be crumbling away. When her parents had died and her sister had left town, St. Nick's had filled her need to be needed, and now Dr. Bailey was saying everything would run smoothly without her? Oh, no, no, no! Wait. The twins! Her sister was coming back. She couldn't go. No. She wouldn't leave.

"What about my sister? She needs me!"

"When is she coming?"

Honesty forced an answer. "Ten...maybe twelve weeks from now? But I have to change so much in the house. Child-proofing...washing sheets..." Even she knew she was waffling now.

Dr. Bailey slung a fatherly arm across her shoulders as she snatched Matteo's sock from her filing cabinet and stuffed it in her pocket. "Plenty of time to go to Buenos Aires and come back again. We'll miss you, of course—but change does a person the world of good sometimes."

"I can't wait!" she squeaked through a frozen smile. Nothing like a bit of change.

Harriet was feeling an awful lot like Maria von Trapp.

Casita Verde's flagship center was big. Grand, actually. And here she was, standing outside, suitcase in hand, with an endless stream of questions yet to be answered and absolutely no ability to play the guitar or make dresses out of drapery. So perhaps a bit less like Maria von Trapp than she'd originally thought.

At this juncture? She was willing to try… Or to run after the taxi driver and beg him to take her back to the airport.

She tilted her head back and looked up. She wasn't quite sure what she'd expected, but an enormous stone edifice with beautiful tile mosaics of trees, flowers and other happy-making shapes hadn't exactly been what had popped into her mind. The huge front door was a deep green. Like Matteo's eyes.

Her stomach churned.

If she'd had any confidence in her singing she might've burst into some sort of plucky song in a vain attempt to give herself courage or confidence or whatever it was she needed in order to reach out and press the brass buzzer.

Why, why why had she agreed to this?

She was supposed to be at home, finishing up baby-proofing the house for her sister. Only six tiny little weeks to go before she would officially be an aunt, and she was here in the land of tango and voracious carnivores? And Matteo.

She gave herself a little shake.

She'd be home in four weeks so she would still have time for the finishing touches but… She took in a deep breath. *How does* air *smell different?* She shook her head in disbelief. Being here was something she'd never, ever in a million squillion years imagined herself doing.

Then again, quite a few things had been falling into that category lately. Having naughty sex in her office with just about the most amazing man she'd ever met was pretty close to topping the charts at this juncture. Her body responded with a shivery reminder of just how nice it had been. Not that she'd heard so much as a whisper from Matteo since he'd disappeared That Night. *What a confidence builder!*

Not that she'd expected daily contact. They'd made no promises to one another and certainly she'd never expected to see him again. It was probably one of the reasons she'd been so brazen That Night. Who was fooling who here? It was all the brazen she had! And using it all up in one go when she wouldn't need it anymore? Not the sharpest of moves.

When she'd received Matteo's invitation, via Dr. Bailey, to work at Casita Verde, it had been as if all the oxygen had been sucked out of her body and replaced with helium. She hadn't even been able to answer. She had just nodded. A lot. Matteo wanted to see her again.

And then…nothing.

Unless you counted a politely worded informational PDF sent via "Administrator" with no personal add-ons other than a reminder that it was winter in Buenos Aires so she'd best pack a warm coat and summer clothes as the weather was variable. She'd harrumphed at the computer.

At least "Administrator" had cared if she got frostbite.

And she'd said as much to the non-English-speaking taxi driver on her way into Buenos

Aires after thanking the heavens she'd printed out the address of Casita Verde in large print on a huge piece of paper. Preparedness was key when you had no idea what was coming. Two weeks of intensive Spanish classes weren't all they were cracked up to be.

"I doubt he even knows I'm arriving today." Harriet had begun, her voice not particularly audible above the blare of a tango song filling the cab. At least it had made talking to herself less embarrassing.

"Dr. Bailey probably made the entire thing up to see if I was brave enough to leave St. Nick's for the first time in, well, forever. It was almost like he didn't want me there! He practically booted me out the door!" She'd given her best astonished face in the direction of the rear-view mirror and continued, the taxi driver taking no notice of her whatsoever.

"I mean, honestly! I really needed at least— *at least*—a month, maybe two, to hand over everything to the staff nurses, and what did he give me?" She'd looked into the rearview mirror again, half expecting to see an eyebrow lifting with curiosity.

Nothing.

The driver had been too engrossed in his radio sing-along. *Typical.* Sign number two she shouldn't have boarded the plane. Not beyond passport control more than half an hour and already she was invisible.

She carried on.

"Three weeks! Can you believe it? Three weeks to hand over a decade's worth of diligence. Or… well…a lot of years. And diligence. And having no life, even though that part might be my fault. But seriously? What does he think I am? A pair of castanets on overdrive?" She gave the rear-view mirror another indignant look. She was on a roll now.

The car lurched and Harriet's hands flew to her stomach. She'd been sick on the plane and had put it down to nerves—but as the car zigzagged through the thick morning traffic she was beginning to wonder if she didn't suffer a bit from motion sickness. She blew her breath into her hand and sniffed. Thank goodness for that little toothbrush and toothpaste they give you on the plane. The driver unleashed a flurry of what she expected were ruby-colored unpleasantries as a lorry all but took the front of the taxi off. *Sign number three?*

"You want to take a guess at what Dr. Bailey said when I protested?" Harriet didn't bother pausing. This was obviously a soliloquy and she was going to make the most of it.

"Go on! Get out of here and go buy yourself something *Argentinian* to wear! Whatever that might be. It's not like the streets of London are flooded with...with whatever Argentinians wear."

Her voice petered out with her confidence so she pressed her nose against the window finally taking in all the sights and sounds she hadn't even begun to imagine. Including floods of sleek-looking ebony-haired Argentinian women looking all sexy and chic while she just felt rumpled and jet-lagged.

A sting of tears threatened as the newness of it all hit her.

When Dr. Bailey had all but shooed her out of the office she hadn't known whether to laugh or cry. He'd practically chased her out of the ward as if she'd been a bad smell. So what if she was a homebody? Or, more accurately, a St. Nick's body. She loved it there. It was her life! And, from the looks of things, her "all" hadn't been enough for her boss and mentor.

"There's more to life than St. Nick's has to offer!"

Those were Dr. Bailey's words that had felt the stabbiest. Akin to betrayal.

When her parents had died ten years ago she'd shifted from useful daughter to useful sister. Claudia had taken their parents' death as a cue to grab life voraciously by the collar and shake as much fun, passion, and drama out of it as she could. "If I go down? I want to be in a plane flying across the savannah of Africa, too! I am going to go down sucking the very marrow out of life!"

In fact, when she'd rung Claudia to tell her about her ignominious booting out, her twin had all but offered to trade places. Her voice had lowered and gone all *are-you-freakin'-kidding-me?* on her. "A month with a sexy Latin doctor in Buenos Aires? You'd be mad not to go!"

"But what about the house? About my job? About your twins?"

"What about them?" Claudia had asked, as if jumping on the plane was a done deal. "I'm not due for weeks yet and won't be flying with them straight out of the womb. Chill!"

Too much California or just plain nutter?

Then again, what else was it her sister had said? She ran a finger over the door's buzzer as if it were a magic eight ball. "Finally!" Her sister's voice reverberated through her memory. "Acting from your heart and not that overactive head of yours!"

Little tingles of delight shimmied through her tummy as if to back up her sister's words. It was true that when she'd been with Matteo it had felt incredibly...liberating.

Tears swooped into her eyes as she stared at the brass doorbell some more.

No-o-o-o!

This was not how she wanted Matteo to see her. It would be, she imagined, exactly the scenario he had anticipated. Why he'd put "Administrator" in charge of her welcome. She was a nerdy, change-resistant, too-fragile-to-take-it-on-the-chin research nurse.

She turned away from the epically huge wooden door and shook her head, willing the emotions squeezing at her chest, her throat, her eyes to leave her be. Give her a moment's respite to be brave. She stamped her feet and gave her shoulders a shake.

C'mon, Harriet. Channel your sister if you have to, but you did not just spend twenty hours having a four-year-old kick the back of your seat only to go running back home with your tail between your legs. It is time for you to stand on your own two feet!

"*¡Cuidado!*"

Harriet's head whipped to the left just in time to see a swarm of children careening towards her at high speed. Her Spanish might not be up to much but she was pretty sure she was being told to get out of the way—and fast.

She took a step back and immediately regretted it. Her foot hit a slick of wet leaves with no intention of staying stationary. Her arms windmilled to gain balance as her knees buckled against the bulk of her suitcase. As she somersaulted over the back of it she felt a microsecond's regret she hadn't brought the one with wheels.

"Whoa!"

Harriet's battle with gravity was being lost in a slow-motion collapse towards the pavement. Her hands hit the ground with a skidding jolt. She was already feeling the abrasion's initial burn as one of her knees took a hit of gravel. Looked like her "good impression skirt" had been a bad idea, then.

There would be a need for tweezers in her immediate future.

What she hadn't expected was such an apocalyptically klutzy landing that she'd received a face full of dirt, more gravel and— Oh… Actually, those were some very nice tiles. What a beautiful blue!

Her eyes remained focused on the ground, but she could hear the children circle her, speaking in rapid-fire Spanish. Her brain was too addled by the fall to make much sense of what they were saying. After a moment's assessment that, no, she hadn't broken anything, she took a slow breath, regrouped and turned herself round to face her spectators.

Standing above her, backlit by a clear blue sky, was none other than… Matteo Torres.

"Harriet! I see you've met the children."

Who made him behave like a bemused Captain Von Trapp? *Had someone sent a memo?*

She pulled her hand away from her face. Could she really feel any more like an idiot?

Well.

She could be naked.

She yanked at the hem of her skirt to make sure she wasn't doing a fresh pair of underwear display to boot.

Her tummy did its own special gymnastics routine. The sexy kind. Who knew her insides were capable of feeling *torrid*? The fuzz of memory shifted into a connection between her eyes and brain. Matteo was offering her a hand up. He did not look amused.

Awkward!

"Thank you. *Gracias*," she mumbled, reaching out her scraped hand with not a little mortification.

"Good to see you have such a command of our native tongue."

Matteo's face was unreadable but she would've put money on his tone: Smug.

"*Bueno verte tambien*, Dr. Torres." Harriet tugged her hand out of his with a sniff.

She hadn't spent the entire flight watching

the Spanish language films without subtitles for nothing. *Y Tu Mama Tambien* that!

She wiped her hand uselessly along her filthy skirt. Jaunty riposte or no, she got the message. Matteo didn't want her here.

Without a second glance at her, she watched as he briskly began dispensing children hither and yon. Some through the big green door, some down around the corner and a couple of youngsters who were... Oh! Picking up her suitcase and her carry-on bags, lugging them through the stone portico into...

Oh... The most beautiful courtyard she thought she'd ever seen in her life. It was...bewitching.

A fire lit in her chest. If she'd not left home, she never would have seen this magical place.

Red terracotta tiles bedecked a covered walkway encircling a large—huge!—central green, dotted here and there with what she guessed were fruit trees, each ringed with gorgeous mosaics made from a mishmash of broken ceramics.

Had the *children* done those? Amazing.

In fact, now that she'd given herself a few moments to take it all in, the entire courtyard was bedecked by one art project after the other. Tables and benches made of reclaimed wood. Were those old pallets made into a tree swing? Genius! Broken bits of mirror, pottery and pebbles bedecked the columns holding up a second-story walkway. It was brilliant. If this place was anything like St. Nick's, there were breakages aplenty. And to turn them into art? Inspired.

A little shiver worked its way along her spine despite the mild winter weather. What did they call the summery winter? *El veranito de San Juan?* The guidebook had warned of it and she'd scrambled to take off her sensible tights on the plane. She chanced a glance at her grubby legs. Who knew she'd need kneepads at the ripe age of twenty-nine?

Hiding her grimace, she continued to soak in the details of the courtyard. It wasn't opulent— wonderfully comforting was more like it. Exactly what she would have done in England if it were more like…right here. Green wooden doors nestled within the walkway, signs on the outside of each door delineating bedrooms, offices and—

"Like what you see?"

Matteo materialized in front of her. Uh. Why, yes, she did, thank you very much, indeed.

The fact she could only nod was probably a giveaway on that front. His dark hair, still a rumpled, silky swatch of perfection, was all but begging to be touched. So close she could see there were shadows beneath those green eyes of his. Her fingers itched to reach out and stroke his cheeks, feel the scratch of his five o'clock shadow making an appearance too early in the day. He turned to face the courtyard, reminding her she was meant to be commenting on the casita.

"Beautiful." That was all she managed.

"I think you might want to come with me." She felt Matteo's hand press against the small of her back, steering her towards a nearby door with a large red cross on the front of it. She fought the urge to crane her neck and see what his face was doing. Confirm he was as grumpy as he sounded.

Her back gave a little quiver as his fingers shifted a bit closer to her bum when she stepped up into the doorway. Talk about *verboten*! She'd have to have a talk with her body about that. Sexy, sexy, naughty nursey couldn't undo her hairpins here. In fact...sexy, sexy, naughty nursey was someone she thought she'd never see again. Curious. She just managed to catch sight of the door sign before she entered.

Enfermería.

The clinic.

Perfecto! Just the reunion she'd been hoping for! Scraped knees and a stone-faced Matteo in a clinic…about seven thousand miles from anything and everything that was familiar to her. Except medicine. Her tried and true friend.

"You want me to start right away?" she asked hopefully, pushing open the door and scanning the room. *Nice.* Simple, but nice. She was a bit tired, but if popping her into the clinic to keep her out of harm's way was how things were going to be, then she was ready to roll up her sleeves.

"No, you silly goose." Matteo's voice deepened, hinting at the warmth she knew it was capable of. Harriet spied the odd pair of dark eyes darting in and out of the doorway with an accompanying giggle. Children were just as curious here as they were at home. Matteo gave her a self-effacing smirk as he spread out a clean swatch of paper on the exam table. When he moved to ease her up onto the table via a children's footstool— how helpless did he think she was?—his scent flooded her nostrils anew. "I thought we'd see to your cuts and scrapes before you met the boss. He's very strict about welfare. And hygiene."

Why did he have to smell so nice?

"He doesn't seem all that welcoming either," Harriet chanced, presuming they were discussing Matteo in the third person. Which was weird. *He was being weird!* She might be klutzy, but this version of Matteo was not the relaxed, passionate man she'd met less than a month ago. Had it all been an act for funding? The thought didn't sit right. She knew she didn't excel at a lot of things but was certain about her skills at judging a man's character.

She narrowed her eyes and squinted at him. He was busily opening a cabinet and gathering an arsenal of bandages and cleaning agents. "What are you doing? It's only a scraped hand and a knee full of gravel!"

"I'm trying to be civil."

"Civil?" She couldn't help bridling. "How about friendly? Maybe *friendly* would be a nice way to treat someone who's just flown halfway around the world to lend a hand?"

Matteo said nothing. Harriet felt a bit shell-shocked herself. She never spoke out like this. She was mousy, quiet Harriet, not a lippy demander of pleasantries.

"I'm trying to…" he began, then stopped.

"Trying to what?" She was going to go with this demanding-answers vibe that had bubbled up from somewhere she'd never tapped before. It felt good to speak so openly. So freely. "Why not issue me with a whistle and a set of guidelines and just be done with it? Then you can get on with your life and I can get on with mine."

Matteo pressed his hands into the counter where he'd been laying out anesthetic wipes alongside some tweezers and froze.

So she'd hit the nail on the head. *Terrific!* She'd finally taken a chance—an absolutely bonkers chance that, admittedly, she'd actually been kind of forced to take, but never mind that—and had flown all this way to discover Matteo didn't even want her here. Absolutely brilliant.

She swiped at the tears falling from her eyes. Her feisty say-it-out-loud self was taking a nosedive back into Insecurityville. A fleeting case of false bravura. Nothing more.

She tilted her head up to heaven, grateful Matteo wasn't looking at her. Thankfully, it also helped stem the onset of tears. Every cloud had its silver lining. Right?

"I invited you in a spur-of-the-moment decision." Matteo's eyes were still glued to the counter. He was making a right and utter hash of this. This wasn't how he'd wanted to greet Harriet. Not by a long shot. Hell. Who was he kidding? Fifty percent of him had been hoping she wouldn't come. The other fifty percent?

He turned to face her. *Might as well know the truth.*

Sí. Still sucker-punched by her beauty. By the impact she'd had on him in such a short time. Even if she did have dirt smeared all over her face and grimy hands and knees, like one of the children. Unexpectedly, he started laughing.

"What?" Harriet's purse-lipped response preceded an erratic once-over of her injuries before she hobbled from the table to examine herself in the mirror.

"Why didn't you tell me?" She rounded on him.

Matteo was fully laughing now.

"What? That you look like one of the children who scavenge for garbage?"

"Yes!"

She was irate now—hands on hips, blue eyes wide, open demanding an explanation—and for some reason it fueled his laughter even more.

"Because, *amorcito*..." he stuffed a fist in front of his mouth, trying to fake-cough away his laughter "...you look like an angelic urchin with your blue eyes and blonde hair. The children will think you are from heaven."

His voice trailed off, leaving a silence humming with expectation. It would've been so easy to pull her into his arms. Cup her face in his hands and kiss her sweet rosebud of a mouth. Laughing children and the buzz of activity could be heard out in the courtyard as they stood there, eyes connected to each other's as if they could stay that way forever. But that's not how things worked here. How he worked. Even so...another moment wouldn't hurt.

Slowly, but very surely, he saw the puff of indignation in her deflate. A smile started to tease at her lips, gradually climbing into her eyes. Unexpectedly, she too began to laugh.

"It looks like I'll have a shiner by the end of the day. Whatever day it is. Is it Sunday or Monday?"

"It's Monday, *chuchura*. You must be exhausted. Come here." He patted the exam table. "Up you get."

He might have been using the same words he would with one of the children, but when she slipped up onto the table, and he pulled his wheelie stool over so that he was in prime position to pluck the grit out of her knee, image after image of their night in her office flooded his mind, making it virtually impossible to focus.

"Scraped knees aren't contagious, you know."

"I know. I am just thinking of the best approach."

"For a scraped knee?" Harriet wasn't convinced by his peculiar expression. "Do you want me to do it? Give me the tweezers."

"No! Not unless you want to do it. I've got things to do."

What was he doing? Playing medical table tennis?

"If I'm keeping you from something…" Her defenses flew up at the increasing level of testiness in his voice.

"No! No." He forced himself to level his tone. "You're good. I'm good. We're all good."

Harriet tipped her chin to the side and shot him a dubious look.

"Somehow I don't quite believe you."

What could he say to that? She was absolutely right. The fact that she was here had upended everything. And it wasn't exactly as if he could say that, could he? He'd been the one to invite her here and now he was giving her the cold shoulder?

He was going to have to face facts. Having Harriet here would challenge everything he'd set so solidly in stone after his sister had died. And he didn't want things challenged. Wasn't ready for change. And yet…it had been his invitation that had brought her here.

He barked out a hollow laugh into the tiled room. What was it his mother always said? If you ask, then you shall receive?

"Harriet, I—I need you to know I don't normally have…" He opened his eyes a bit wider as if it was some sort of magical code for one-night stands.

"What? And you think I do?"

Apparently it was.

"No—not at all." He didn't. Not in the slightest. What had happened between them had been special. Singular. He knew it in his very core. He hoped she knew it. But saying as much could mean opening the doors to further possibility and that's not how he worked. How life worked.

"Because if that's what you think of me, then you can just think yourself right out of that thought." She gave him a prim nod and pressed her hands against the exam table as if to dismount then stopped herself, as he was directly blocking her exit route. "You know what?" She started over with a brusque shake of her head, blonde hair forming a halo round her face. "Don't worry. You don't have to say it."

"You don't even know—"

She held up a hand to stop him. "Yes, I do. I might not get the wording exactly right, but you want what happened between us to be…what *happened* between us. *Niente. Nada. Nul.* No more. I know. I get it."

She had more courage than he did. Saying out loud the words that coming from him would sound so…so arrogant! Dismissive, even.

A twist of self-loathing shot through him. She didn't deserve this.

"I can't offer you what you want."

"How do you even know what I want?"

Her expression was defiant. Defensively so. Had he meant something to her in so short a time? Stupid question.

She wasn't someone who had casual sex. Neither was he. And she meant something to him. That's why he was doing this. Setting boundaries. To keep both of their lives in order.

At least that's what he would keep telling himself.

He clapped his hands in a let's-get-going way and took up the pair of tweezers. "Shall we get you cleaned up so you can meet the children?"

"Absolutely." He watched as she forced on a bright smile. "The children are why I'm here. Aren't they, Dr. Torres?"

CHAPTER FIVE

HARRIET STABBED THE long number into her mobile, knowing her phone bill would be about a trillion pounds when she got home, but she didn't care. She needed a dose of Claudia. Strong-willed, deeply passionate, problem-conquering Claudia. She gave her freshly bandaged knee a rub. Staring at Matteo as he had plucked the bits of gravel out of her as if she were a rascally five-year-old had been a test. The first of many, she imagined.

As the click and whir of the number began to go through, she suddenly noticed the time. It was still morning in Buenos Aires and Argentina was well ahead of Los Angeles. Being overtired wasn't something she wanted to add to Claudia's list of pregnancy woes. She probably already had fatigue mastered without an insecure sister unleashing a stream of worries on her. No. Check that. Harriet wasn't insecure—she was just over-whelmed with "new."

"New" was Claudia's specialty. Same old, same old was Harriet's. They balanced one another. The yin to the other's yang. Or whichever way round that was meant to work. Claudia would be the exciting-as-they-come mother and she'd be the reliable auntie.

A shot of excitement at her impending auntie-hood brought a smile to her lips as she pressed the hang-up symbol. Six weeks, two days and a handful of hours from now she would be Auntie to two little boys! Who would, no doubt, be gorgeous, like their mother.

Their mother, who was in stupid Los Angeles, not helping her out of this stupid mess with Mr. Stupid right here in the heart of Stupidville.

Not that she was a grown woman or anything who could sort out her own problems. Right?

A little moan of self-pity escaped her lips as she leant back on the wooden bench she'd found tucked away in this far corner of the courtyard. She traced a finger along a thick plank. It, like most of the furniture she'd seen, looked solid. Well crafted. Beautiful.

One of Matteo's resources?

No doubt. She imagined he had fingers in all sorts of fruitful pies.

An image of him lifting a forkful of glossy cherry pie in her direction sped across her brain.

That wasn't going to get her anywhere, was it?

She tried to cut the image into bits with each lazy swing of the overhead fan. Chop. Chop. Chop.

Not working! Picturing an imaginary Matteo being obliterated by the world's slowest ceiling fan was not a problem solver.

Frustration began to nibble away at her already frayed nerve endings. Why did Matteo have to be so…so…? So… *Matteo*?

She was going to have to regroup. Block That Night from her mind. It, after all, wasn't the reason she'd leapt onto a plane as if it were the beginning of a magical rainbow-laced journey.

The reason she'd come was because of Casita Verde's children and the good that would come of a new clinic. Nothing to do with the dark-haired, golden-tanned, green-eyed hunk of gorgeousness who ran it. The one who'd run his hands just about everywhere over her naked body before—

Stop it.

Fantasizing about what had been didn't make right now any better.

A flash of irritation shot through her. One acknowledging that Matteo was right.

If they were busy having a delicious romance, all of their time, all of their *energy* wouldn't be going to the children. St. Nick's was making an investment in her. In her work. And if she came up trumps, Casita Verde would get a new clinic and she could go home to follow exactly the same routine she'd been following quite happily for her entire adult life. Back to the status quo in no time. Just what she wanted. So! Harriet shook her head and forced on a smile, Operation Crush the Crush was going to have to be put in motion.

An unexpected rush of children into the courtyard brought her to her feet. She saw a woman being ushered in and— Oh, no!

Harriet quickly wove her way through the children to reach the heavily pregnant woman's side. She was young. Teenager young. Fifteen, sixteen maybe? And letting out the most extraordinary howl of pain Harriet thought she had ever heard. Her arms, legs, face…everything about her looked unnaturally swollen.

Pre-eclampsia. It had to be. Common in teen-aged pregnancies. The only way to prevent the swelling from causing this woman's death was to deliver the child immediately.

She took hold of the young woman's arm and steered her the handful of steps up into the clinic.

"Cómo te llamas?"

"Carlita," the young woman managed to gasp.

"Carlita. That's a lovely name. *Hablo Ingles?*" Harriet wasn't going to risk her limited Spanish on an emergency like this if she didn't have to. She scanned the courtyard, which suddenly felt as large as an aircraft hangar.

Where was Matteo? She asked a couple of young boys to find him.

"Sí." She began again after blowing a steadying breath through tightly pursed lips, "Yes, I studied it in school."

"I'm just bringing you to the clinic. How far along are you?"

"Maybe thirty-six weeks. I'm not sure."

Harriet winced. Carlita very likely hadn't been receiving check-ups. Thirty-six weeks was early but not too risky. Any earlier than that and the child could face severe medical issues.

"How long have you been having contractions?"

"Bring her in here." Matteo materialized in the doorway, the expression on his face completely devoid of light as his eyes hit Carlita. This was a side to him she hadn't seen. Her heart clenched tight. There was something personal in his response to the young woman.

He indicated they enter a room Harriet hadn't seen yet. When he swung the door open her eyes widened.

"Were you saving this as a surprise for later?"

"I was saving it," Matteo replied matter-of-factly, "for someone who was about to give birth."

The immaculately maintained obstetrics room might not have had every single bell and whistle but it was well equipped enough to handle, at the very least, straightforward situations.

"Can you get a urine sample and then prep her on the table, please? I just need to make a quick call." Matteo had a phone tucked between his chin and shoulder as he scanned the medicine cabinet.

"Are you happy to give an intramuscular injection?"

"Of course." Harriet tried not to take offense at his tone. This was an emergency. Not the time to quarrel about how much she could and couldn't do.

"Magnesium sulfate?" she asked as he began speaking in rapid Spanish.

He nodded and handed over the syringe, mouthing, "Four grams in an IV," as he listened to the response before hanging up and going back to the medicine cupboard.

"Gloves are over there." Matteo pointed at well-stocked box in the corner.

She snapped on a pair and gave the teen a smile. "Carlita, do you know if you have HIV?"

"I'm okay."

"Excellent." At least that wouldn't be a problem the teen would have to deal with in addition to a newborn.

Matteo cut in, "One of my colleagues—friends—from a local hospital is coming to help. The more hands the better."

Harriet nodded, swabbing Carlita's hand after hanging the IV bag on a nearby stand. She gave the teen her best reassuring smile and said, "This won't hurt too much," before slipping the needle into her hand after injecting the magnesium sulfate into the IV bag. It wasn't a cure-all and would take five to ten minutes to be given via infusion pump, but it would help prevent convulsions. Essential if they were to hope for a positive outcome.

"Hydralazine?" Harriet asked when Matteo handed her another syringe.

"Yes. For the blood pressure. We'll start with ten milligrams and see how she's doing in ten minutes. Could be it needs to be injected intravenously."

"Fluid regimen?"

"What happened with the urine test?" Matteo's eyes scanned the room as if it could answer.

"I didn't test it."

Matteo shot her a dark look. *Calm. Calm. Be the calm in the storm.*

"She's only just arrived and I don't know where the dipsticks are."

His expression softened.

There was some understanding in there. Somewhere. Besides, an emergency birth wasn't the place for egos. Pure concentration was the only solution.

Matteo began asking Carlita questions in a slow, steady voice as he slipped the blood-pressure sleeve gently along her swollen arm.

Harriet was pleased to realize she was able understand a lot more Spanish than she could speak. At least she wouldn't be completely in the dark.

"Have you had any seizures?"

"One. That is why I came."

"You were already in labor?"

"I don't know." Her eyes widened with fear. "What is going to happen to my baby?"

"BP is one fifty over ninety-five." Matteo met Harriet's eyes with a modicum of relief as he took off the sleeve. If it had been higher—one-seventy over one hundred and ten?—Carlita's chances of a cerebral hemorrhage would have been increased. As would the likelihood of death for both mother and child.

"Headaches? Blurred vision? How long have your ankles been this swollen?"

Matteo rattled off the questions and Carlita stumbled through her answers as they worked in unison to prepare for delivery. They would need to lower her blood pressure—but not too rapidly, otherwise they risked an acute reduction in the flow of blood and oxygen to the placenta.

"Can you test her reflexes?" Matteo handed Harriet the small instrument as he continued the flow of questions. Abdominal pain? An absence of or reduced urine over the past few hours? Days? They were all clues that, had she been receiving regular prenatal check-ups, would have prevented the severity of her case. Matteo's face was grim.

"Can you cut off her clothes, please? We need to check the baby."

"Of course, Doctor."

Matteo shot her a look. One that was impossible to read. What did he expect? It was hardly the place to call him lover boy. Not that she'd ever, ever call him that.

A sharp rap sounded on the door and a middle-aged man wearing scrubs entered without waiting for a response.

"Matteo." He gave him a quick nod followed up by a questioning look when he saw Harriet.

"Harriet, this is Dr. Morales, an obstetrician from Hospital de los Porteños. He will help us with the delivery. Carlita? How are you feeling?" Matteo's attention returned to Carlita, whose eyes suddenly rolled up behind her lids.

"She's seizing." Harriet's words were lost in the flurry of action that followed.

After checking her airway, breathing and circulation, Harriet helped stabilize Carlita's head and upper body as Dr. Morales administered an additional magnesium sulfate bolus of two grams.

"Do you think we need to use a prophylactic?" Harriet asked. It had been a while since she'd been in a delivery room, but everything she knew was flooding back at a rate of knots.

"Let's hold off and see how she goes. It could be that her labor has progressed enough that we can deliver," Dr. Morales replied. "Matteo? How is it looking?"

"She's already dilated to eight centimeters. Want to wait until ten?"

"I'm not getting much of a read on the baby. Episiotomy?"

Harriet winced when she realized Carlita saw her flinch at the word. An episiotomy would speed things up and with proper anesthetics she wouldn't feel the cut at all. On top of which, the sooner she had the child, the better. The only way to stop pre-eclampsia from taking both of their lives was delivery of the child.

She took the young woman's hand in hers and held it tight. Where was Carlita's family? It must be so frightening to be alone like this.

She looked across at Matteo and Dr. Morales, who were working together like a well-oiled machine. Their exchanges were brief but explanatory. Harriet kept an eye on the obs as they prepped both themselves and Carlita for the delivery, talking her through each step of the journey. Any darkness Matteo's eyes had carried earlier had lifted, leaving behind the kind, confident doctor she had first met. This was the man she'd heard about for so many years, the one who offered girls a place of refuge, help in a time of critical need.

"It's okay." She spoke quietly into Carlita's ear as they prepared to make the incision. "You're in good hands."

"Here she is!" Matteo gave the infant a swift wipe to clear away any blood and mucus before expertly swaddling her in a light green blanket.

"Look!" He held the tiny infant outstretched in his arms. "We've had a baby."

He'd meant to look at Carlita when he said the words, gave the smile. It was his standard line, but he meant it every time he said it. Especially in cases like this when such a critical medical situation ended with both mother and baby in good shape. Alive. But as he spoke, his body betrayed him and his eyes solidly latched onto Harriet's.

We've had a baby.

Harriet's lips parted, her eyes widened then clamped tight shut for a moment as if to regroup. No wonder!

The words—usually just a warm welcome for an infant and a "well done" for an exhausted new mother—were suddenly weighted with meaning.

He'd vowed never to have children of his own. It was why this was always the first and last time he held a woman's child. His fingers suddenly ached to hand the child over. What they'd just been through was a vivid reminder of his vow. Matteo's sister and her child had died from preeclampsia, his sister too frightened by her own pregnancy to seek prenatal treatment. Carlita, he had little doubt, was the same. It was why Casita

Verde existed. To try and allow other families' daughters not to become a statistic, the kind that ended with a funeral.

"Do you want to hold her?"

Harriet's eyes lit up as Matteo handed the baby across so that she could pass the infant to Carlita.

Something in him softened as he handed over the tiny, wriggling parcel, already complete with a head of thick, dark hair. He shifted his hands away from Harriet's arms as she took the weight of the baby and again became acutely aware of the connection between them. And not just on a physical level.

She'd more than impressed him today.

Without a thought for herself she had jumped straight in at the deep end, still exhausted from her journey and no doubt wondering where the hell the man who had made love to her with untethered desire had gone. The one who had *invited* her here and all but cast her aside in the first five minutes.

And here she was, nurturing and supporting someone with utter focus, as if Carlita was the very first new mother in the world. It took a generosity of spirit not everyone possessed. Yes, it was her job. But she did it well. Very well. That much was clear. He added another tick to her list of good qualities.

Harriet ran a finger along the infant's face, the instinct to nurture coming to the fore before she turned to Carlita.

"Meet your daughter."

"Do I have to?" Carlita's pained voice broke the spell.

Harriet looked across at Matteo, unsure what to do. The baby let out a small cry and they all turned to look. Harriet's arms automatically began an instinctive rocking motion. A lullaby, just audible above the whir of an outdoor generator, came in a low hum from her lips.

"Carlita, *mija*." Matteo moved to the opposite side of the bed. "There is no 'have to' here. You know that. But I think it might be a good idea."

"Why?"

He could feel Harriet's eyes on him. She didn't really know his style yet and would be seeing first hand how he liked to handle things at Casita Verde.

"I think it is important to say hello," he began, drawing Carlita's hand between both of his and giving it a squeeze. "*Gracias* and *adios*." Something he'd never had a chance to say to his sister or her child. And the reason he never cuddled or cooed at an infant. Ten years on it was still too painful. Too raw.

"Thank you?"

"*Sí*. You are very, very lucky. You almost lost your life today. And your child might have too, but she was smart enough to know you needed to go into labor straight away." He gave a soft smile. "You haven't had any prenatal appointments, have you?"

"Not exactly." Her eyes began darting anxiously around the room.

"There's no one here to judge you, Carlita. We are here to help you. But what happens now is largely up to you."

"I know. But she is going to have a good home, so it's all right! I don't need to hold her."

"Which home?" Matteo's voice intensified. They'd not met Carlita before today and, as far as he knew, she'd not been to the other clinics.

"Here. That's what you do, right? You'll find her a nice home and my parents will never have to know." She began to push herself up, her body and mind still clearly under the light haze of anesthetics.

"No, you don't, darling." Harriet pressed a hand on Carlita's shoulder. "You need rest now. And plenty of it." She gave her a smile. "How are we going to monitor your blood pressure, your *health*, if you don't stay for a while?"

"You've got a few days here, *mija*. Not to mention," chipped in Dr. Morales, "we'll need to check your liver for enzymes, thrombocytopenia, hemolytic uremic—"

"Okay!" Carlita waved her hands in the air, desperate for him to stop. "Okay."

Matteo rose from the side of her bed. "We'll transfer you to a more comfortable room where you can rest over the next few days and we can keep an eye on you. We will take care of your baby—but as far as your baby is concerned there is no automatic home. No magic queue of parents waiting outside the door."

Carlita's eyes widened and instantly filled with tears.

"She won't go to someone today?"

"No." He nodded at Harriet, indicating she should hand the baby to Carlita.

"So you have time to say thank you, little one. Thank you for helping to save my life."

"I was the one who came here!" Carlita protested.

"Because you were in labor. If you hadn't been…?" Matteo left the question hanging in the air.

Carlita looked at the baby again, lifted her arms then lowered them, nerves getting the better of her.

"What will holding her do?" Carlita sent Matteo a plaintive look.

"*Aiie—guapita*. Hold her. Just say thank you to *la chiquita*. If you are old enough to make a baby, you are old enough to say thank you to her for saving your life," Matteo rebuked the young woman, but with a smile playing on his lips. She was seventeen. Too young and too worldly in equal parts.

He found this moment in the process difficult. He saw it as helping with the parenting he wished his sister had received. And it was so personal. There was no universally accepted way to deal with each and every teen birth. And how to find that perfect balance? Stern, loving, with a healthy dose of arm's-length understanding?

Carlita looked at her daughter, still being rocked in Harriet's arms, her wary expression shifting to one of awe. The one that made it worth it. The one that helped them *learn*.

"Then we will talk about when to call your parents."

"Que?" There was no mistaking the dismay on Carlita's face.

"Sí. That's right. Adoption can't get underway without approval from a judge and you are going to need their help. I will help, too, but family is important. Now, let's deal with first things first," he continued briskly, before she could get too caught up in all the information she'd just received. "What do you think of this little beauty, eh? She has a nice head of hair, no?"

"*Sí,* Doctor." Carlita gave him a bashful smile before turning to Harriet to receive the expertly wrapped bundle of baby.

"What will happen to them?" Harriet had to run a couple of steps to catch up with Matteo as he crossed the courtyard a couple of hours after the baby and Carlita had been settled and they'd said farewell to Dr. Morales.

The sunny, smiling doctor had all but disappeared when they'd left the delivery room. In his stead she saw a man wrestling with something. Balance in a world that would never make sense?

Her question remained unanswered.

"Is that pretty standard?" Harriet tried to match his long, swift strides.

"They're all different. This is one of the good ones, believe it or not. There will be a bit of a process with the courts to get the child made ready for adoption. Nothing we haven't dealt with before. It all takes time. Patience." He snapped the last word as if she'd been hounding him.

Charming! Especially considering all she was doing was trying to work out how things ran, see where she would best fit in for next few weeks.

Out of the way, from the look of things. Rendering this entire journey pointless.

"Shall I just leave you to it, then?" Harriet stopped walking, her voice sounding more confident than she felt. "Now that I've played my part in your good deed of the day?"

Where had that come from?

Her fingers automatically went to rub her locket. Pictures of her sister and her parents were in there—a never-ending source of courage. They would've been impressed to see her so full of gumption. As well she should be!

Matteo was being cagey. And he wasn't being fair. She crossed her arms in front of her chest, waiting, watching for Matteo to stop his purposeful striding and pay her the common courtesy she had paid him when he had come to visit St. Nick's.

A little flush crept onto her cheeks. If you didn't count spending the best part of two weeks hiding in the patients' rooms to avoid him. She giggled at her schoolgirl behavior.

"So you think this is all funny, do you?" Matteo wheeled round to face her, green eyes dark with emotion.

The irritation in his voice startled her. She hadn't meant to offend and certainly didn't expect this sort of behavior from him. What was going on?

"Of course not." She stayed silent, arms slipping to her sides along with her courage.

He raked a hand through his hair and looked

up at the blue sky above them before tipping his head down, eyes meeting hers. "I'm not really rolling out the proverbial welcome carpet as I had intended."

"Have I done something wrong?"

"No! Absolutely not. It's just…"

"Just…" she softly encouraged. She needed to know, otherwise there was little point in staying. And in that instant—just imagining picking up her suitcase to leave—she already knew she wanted to stay.

"These situations are complicated."

"I do work in an orphanage." She fought the urge to cross her arms. Protect herself. "One filled with dying children, so I'm pretty used to complicated."

"Of course you are. It's just… I have a particular way of dealing with the girls. You're going to see a lot of things that are done very differently."

"So? I thought the point of my being here was exactly that. To expand my horizons." She lobbed the words he'd used at her reluctance to leave London straight back at him. If they were going to have this talk? They were going to have this talk.

"What's so different about what you do anyhow? All I saw was a doctor who saved a teenage girl from dying after safely delivering her child. Then you asked her to acknowledge a few facts about the situation."

"*Sí.* Yes, I know what you saw." He gave her a look that practically screamed, *Isn't it obvious what you're missing?*

Er...no!

"I'm afraid you're going to have to spell it out for me, Matteo."

"I'm just not used to being scrutinized."

"What?" Harriet looked round the courtyard as if hoping to garner some support. "Is that what you feel I've been doing? *Scrutinizing* you? I thought I was just doing what you asked me to do."

"You did, you were. Are." The words piled on top of each other as if he was trying to find just the right one.

"Then what is it? What have I done?"

He crossed to her and placed a hand on her shoulder. She shrugged it off. He didn't get to play nicey-nicey in the throes of this type of conversation.

He took a step back, hands raised as if admitting to an error of judgment. "You've done nothing, *dulce*. It's me. As I said, I'm just not used to being judged."

He turned to go. Harriet was shaking her head. No. This wasn't right. He was speaking in riddles or covering up something deeper. Something that meant more. She couldn't just let this go.

"Is that what you think I'm doing?" she called after him. "That I've flown in from my fancy hospital in London to sanctimoniously *judge* you?"

"No, Harriet—you're getting the wrong idea."

"Then how about explaining to me the right idea? Because from where I'm standing it seems you're the one doing the bulk of the judging here."

Unexpectedly, a broad smile replaced the tight-lipped frown dominating Matteo's face. "Miss Monticello has called the spade a spade!" The light returned to his eyes—the spark of a challenge or the warm glow of acquiescence? It was difficult to tell and she wasn't entirely sure if she should trust it. He beckoned for her to follow him. "Come. Come with me."

Harriet had to force herself to pick up her feet

and follow him. She didn't much feel like jumping back on the Dr. Torres Yo-Yo ride.

He'd already made it perfectly clear where she stood with him personally. Absolutely nowhere. And if he was just going to give her the runaround professionally, there wasn't much point in standing around calling spades much of anything.

Matteo was obviously King of the Mountain here. As he would and should be. Casita Verde was his dream child. He did the work, he secured the funding and he was more hands on than most administrators would ever dream of.

But she was hardly the first person to cross into the courtyard who wanted to know how it worked. Particularly when she was here to roll up her sleeves and help. She knew for a fact he'd had donors, visitors, people "inspecting" before. Surely there was a ream of government departments that had to come in with their clipboards, pens poised to pass judgment, ensure he was doing things to a certain standard. Had he never had anyone come along just to good old-fashioned *help*?

What had made him so touchy about a tiny little *giggle*? A self-deprecating one at that.

Not that he had bothered to ask. She marched along behind him, staring at his back. An annoyingly nice back, his shoulders filling out a dark blue linen shirt as if it had been made for him. Her eyes shifted lower…then a little lower. She humphed under her breath.

He was lucky that staring at his backside was such a pleasant affair, otherwise she had a good mind to hightail it back to the airport. Maybe her sister would need her in Los Angeles…

Matteo kept checking behind him to ensure Harriet was following. Not that he would have blamed her if she'd turned on her heel and left. She was absolutely right. He was the one being difficult. Negative.

He'd had scores of people come to Casita Verde who'd wished to donate but had wanted to "see before they bought". It was completely natural. Fair, even. And normally he never gave a monkey's. If they gave, they gave. If they didn't, he'd carry on. His way. What was so different about Harriet's visit?

Well, that one was easy.

Harriet.

She was what was different.

He cared what she thought and it scared him. He had been moved when handing over the tiny infant and watching her hold it in her arms, the glow of happiness shifting from her to the child as fluidly as if it had been her own.

And seeing that pure, organic, joy…joy he would never know…brought back the endless stream of questions he tortured himself with about his sister. What if there had been somewhere she could go? What if she'd seen a doctor just once and had been warned of the dangers? It physically hurt each time he laid himself bare to the thoughts and now Harriet was seeing the side of himself he worked so hard to keep private. The side he had hoped to keep away from the people he cared about.

Maintaining a blinkered, passionate commitment to what he believed when no one else's opinion mattered was one thing, but now? He wanted Harriet to admire what he'd done. He wanted her to admire *him*. And when she'd laughed? He'd taken it the wrong way. He knew he had and he could *thunk* himself on the head for being so hypersensitive.

Carlita's story, ultimately, would very likely be a successful one. But it was one of thousands and, despite his desire to protect her, Harriet needed to see that many of the children born here, not to mention their young mothers, were not so lucky.

They reached the very back of the compound—not a word passing between them—and he stood for a moment in front of the door, wondering if he was being entirely fair. The turmoil he was feeling was of his own making, but any decisions Harriet made would also stem from what he did now. If she wanted to see what made him so intense, too earnest perhaps, she needed to see this.

He pushed opened the big wooden doors and watched as Harriet's eyes all but turned into saucers. One of the many *villas miserias* of Buenos Aires had crept and crawled, expanding with a speed that almost frightened him, up to the very doorstep of the historic monastery that was now Casita Verde. These were just some of Argentina's impoverished, scraping a living from the nation's capital in any way they could. They lived in huts, lean-tos, under the open sky—anywhere they were able to, doing anything they could to survive.

There was never a chance he'd be able to help a fraction of them, let alone fully open the doors to one and all. Which was why he stayed so focused on teenaged mothers. And why he had to maintain that cool, distanced focus. Letting Harriet into his heart wouldn't help.

He watched her take it in. The children wearing scraps of T-shirts, torn skirts, too-short trousers. The mothers kneading the day's empanada dough in front of fires made of bits of wood scavenged from who knew where. The sprawl—the expanse of it—was breathtaking, even to him, and he saw it every day.

"We solved one problem today," he said, "but out here lie countless more."

"Well, then." Harriet fixed him with her clear blue eyes, her gaze unwavering. "I guess we'd better get to work."

CHAPTER SIX

HARRIET JUST MANAGED to dodge out of the way to avoid a high-speed game of tag weaving in and out of the courtyard's covered walkway. School was finished for the day and the casita's dozen or so school-aged children were burning off some excess energy. She laughed with sheer delight. Matteo might be all frowny and furrowed brow around them—all of them!—but the atmosphere he fostered was definitely child friendly. She had to give him that. She swerved again, her arm getting a silky whiplash from a pair of plaits streaming behind a beautiful eight-year-old girl.

"Mind the—"

"Ow!"

Too late. Camila, in looking behind her, had done a first-class crash into one of the walkway's columns. Harriet was by her side in an instant. Stone columns weren't very forgiving.

"Let's have a look, love." Harriet swept away a

thick swatch of black fringe from the little girl's face, only just stopping herself from wincing. One fat lip, a bloody nose and a good old-fashioned shiner coming up. "I think you and I are going to have something in common!" Harriet put on a smile.

"What?" sniffled Camila.

Harriet pointed at her own fading black eye. "You're going to get one of these!"

Camila stopped crying long enough to give Harriet a shy grin and sweep a hand across her mouth, only to discover it was covered in blood from her streaming nose. Her eyes widened in horror and the tears began anew.

"It's all right, Camila. No—no don't tip your head back. It makes you swallow the blood." Harriet made her best icky face and took one of the little girl's hands. "Can you pinch your nose or would you like me to?"

"I can do it," Camila whimpered.

"Good girl."

"Why don't you vagabonds go and see if Juanita needs some help peeling vegetables?" Matteo's voice came loud and clear from the clinic doorway. The children responded instantly.

When Matteo spoke, everyone listened. Too bad he didn't seem keen on speaking with her. Harriet's lips pressed together as she steered Camila towards the clinic.

Matteo had been doing a most excellent job of keeping Harriet as far away as possible from him and the clinic for the past week. She'd unexpectedly been fighting some serious jet-lag and a bit of a tummy bug so didn't mind too much. Fighting fatigue was one thing, but wrestling with her insecurities was growing more challenging...in the kitchen, the laundry, the children's rooms, the public rooms. Anywhere but in the clinic with Matteo. "All to get you better acquainted with how things work," he'd said. She'd kept her expression neutral with each assignment before accepting it with a smile. He'd run out of ways to keep her out of the clinic soon enough, she'd reasoned. And it looked like patience was rewarding her today.

"Mind the step." Harriet led Camila up the wide stone slabs leading up and into the clinic.

"One bloody nose and a possible black eye coming up!"

Harriet realized she wasn't just speaking to

Matteo but a young woman as well. Almost painfully thin, she was visibly pregnant—perhaps a few months —and sitting in the room's only chair with her arm by the blood-pressure cuff. Must've been a check-up.

"Oops." She turned back to Camila, whose blood was now pooling on the floor. "You've got to keep hold of that nose for a good ten minutes, love. Can—?"

"Shall I...?" Matteo's patient moved to get up, gasping with pain as her legs and hips took her standing weight. She pressed her hands to the arms of the chair for support.

"No, you don't," Matteo interjected, putting a hand on her shoulder. "You stay put." He turned and pulled a length of blue toweling off a rack and grabbed some antiseptic spray, making quick work of the pool of blood as Harriet went down on her knees to take over the nose-pinching job with a handful of tissues to catch any overflow.

"I want to lie down." Camila was crying again.

"No, love. You can't lie down yet. Not until we stop the bleeding and check everything's all right." Harriet gave the girl's cheek a soft brush with the backs of her fingers as she scanned the small room. The only other place to go was the delivery room and keeping that sterile was essential. The casita's need for a bigger clinic and more exam rooms, was pretty obvious right now. Something she would've understood straight away if Matteo had deigned her worthy to help him out over the past week!

"We'll go next door." Matteo made the decision for her. Surprise, surprise. "You all right to handle this?"

"I think I can just about handle a bloody nose," Harriet couldn't help retorting. She'd been doing a ridiculous amount of tongue biting over the past week, but Matteo was crossing a line now. He had no right to question her nursing skills. She'd worked too hard to let someone—let him— patronize her just because she wasn't on her home turf and he had issues about being judged. She was here to help, for heaven's sake, and he was ruddy well going to get the message if it killed her!

"Fine." Matteo's voice said the opposite—but she had a patient to see to, and so did he. No time for egos. Even someone as bull-headed as he was turning out to be should recognize that.

Harriet held Camila to the side as Matteo removed the blood-pressure cuff from the young woman's arm. Signs of pain shot across her eyes again as she pressed her hands to the chair to rise. Interesting. Unusual. When the woman—girl? —began to walk, Harriet thought it was more of a pronounced waddle than would normally be expected for someone who didn't look to be much past the five-month mark. Her mind whirred and reeled through a catalogue of symptoms and possible afflictions. Could it be osteomalacia? Harriet had never seen an actual case of the brittle-bone disease in a pregnant woman before. It was rare—but it happened. And if... Her eyes scanned from the woman's ashen face to her clenched hands and... No. She was probably just leaping to conclusions, too keen to prove to Matteo she was more useful in the clinic than out.

"Let's get you up on the exam table, shall we?" Harriet rose, finding herself playing out an awkward shifting of one person past the other as they tried to move to their new locations. The limited space found her brushing against first the young woman and then Matteo. The woman stopped for a moment to catch her breath just as Matteo was passing Harriet. Their eyes caught and for the first time since she had arrived Harriet felt that instant click of connection that made everything else fade away. Matteo appealed to her on so many levels and it shook her to realize emotion could have such depth. Such a physical impact. Did he feel the same? She searched his green eyes for answers, not even sure herself what the questions were. Her breath caught in her throat as an urge to touch him threatened to engulf her well-honed common sense.

"'Arriet!" Camila whimpered.

Harriet shook her head and returned her focus to her young charge. One thing she knew for sure. Matteo wouldn't rate anyone who put feelings over their work. Such an arm's-length approach for a man who was so devoted to his cause. She couldn't imagine doing her job without pouring her entire heart into it. How he stayed so reserved was beyond her. She turned just as the door to the delivery room clicked shut. He, it appeared, found it as easy as pie. She pictured throwing a huge cream pie right into his gorgeous, all-knowing face and smiled.

"Now, then, Camila. Let's take a look at your sweet little button nose!"

"Your blood pressure and other stats seem fine, but I'm concerned about the amount of pain you are feeling. It's mostly in your hips, you say?"

"*Sí.* But today I have started feeling tingles in my hands and feet. It's why I came along."

Matteo abstained from launching into his usual speech about how she should've come along the instant she'd learned she was pregnant. He would've been able to supply her with essential vitamin and mineral supplements, information about the pregnancy, started the wheels rolling on the adoption process if that's what she was hoping for. He wished the girls knew the door was open to them at any time. An imagine of Harriet standing in the doorway of the casita, a soft smile playing along her lips as she opened her arms wide in welcome eclipsed his thoughts. Her golden hair, lit by the sun. Those blue eyes of hers— *Mierda!* He shook the picture away.

Focus, man!

Having Harriet here was creating fault lines in a decade's worth of intense single-mindedness.

Without it he wasn't sure he would be able to...
Enough! He took the girl's hand in his, kneading, prodding, trying to see if there was anything
obvious causing the tingles. Shingles, diabetes,
a mini-stroke, all things that could dramatically
affect both her health and her unborn child's. He
mouthed a silent curse as he continued the examination. If she'd come earlier this could've been
prevented but Theresa was here now. It would
have to do.

A soft knock on the door caught his attention.
Locks of Harriet's honey-blonde hair were just
visible in the small opening.

"*Sí?* What is it?"

"Sorry...um...sorry, Dr. Torres. May I have a
quick word?"

"Can't it wait?" His tone was sharp, one he
didn't like to hear coming from himself. Especially in front of a patient.

"No."

There wasn't even a glimmer of a waver in her
tone. He pushed his irritation into his emotional
garbage chute and forced himself to regroup.
Harriet was a nurse who more than understood
medical protocol. She wouldn't have interrupted

unless she'd felt it was necessary. He excused himself to Theresa and walked into the other room where Camila was now lying, head elevated, on the exam table, holding an ice packet to her bruised eye and cuddling a small blanket Harriet had twisted into the shape of a poodle. How did she know how to do that sort of thing?

"Sorry to interrupt." Harriet kept her voice low. "You've probably already got your diagnosis for your patient, but I couldn't help but wondering if she wasn't showing signs of osteomalacia." Her eyes met his, nervous expectation playing across them as she waited for his response. He began to dismiss her suggestion but stopped himself. Tingling hands. A distinct waddle when she walked, often indicative of tiny cracks in her hip bones. Pale skin, making it very likely that the healthy percentage of Vitamin D a person should absorb through the skin wasn't present.

He gave her a curt nod. He should have connected the dots himself. "Good call. I'll make her an appointment at the hospital. We don't have the facilities to do all the mineral tests and X-rays she'll need."

"I'll go along with her, if you like."

Matteo pulled himself up to his full height. The alpha male in him bridled. He was capable of looking after his patients—as he had done for many years—without her help, thank you very much! The pragmatist in him countered that someone needed to be at the clinic. He still wasn't ready to figuratively or literally hand over control to anyone else. This was his baby. His effort to make peace with the past. No one but him could understand how the clinic needed to run to right the wrongs.

"That would be very helpful." He gave a grimace and a nod of assent, then tacked on, "Thank you," to take off the edge.

Just a few more weeks. For the love of all things beautiful! He'd made *love* to this woman not a handful of weeks ago! A moment of weakness when he'd let someone see a glimpse of the man he used to be. He glanced at Harriet again before returning to the delivery room. Confusion played across her features. He needed to stop being such a jerk. None of this was her fault. All his idiotic behavior was rooted deep within him, surfacing too often over the past week. Just a few more weeks. And then she'd be gone. Back in England where— *Dios…* He pressed his forehead briefly on the door before turning to face Theresa. He might like not having Harriet here, but he already knew that having her leave was going to be worse.

"Well?" Matteo looked up from his paperwork without so much as a greeting when Harriet finally returned to the clinic.

It had been a long afternoon at the hospital. Her Spanish was still very basic and communicating via a dictionary and her own limited vocabulary had taken it out of her. She was bushed. A smile and a nice cup of tea would've been incredibly welcoming about now.

"We won't know for at least a day. If not two."

"And Theresa?" Matteo craned his head as if Harriet had been hiding the pregnant girl behind her.

"She's gone back to her dormitory."

"Dormitory?"

"She's at university. Her parents don't know," she added before Matteo had a chance to question her. "I've got her mobile number and a promise that she'll meet me for the results when we get the call." She put up a hand when she saw Matteo was about to interrupt her. *Give a girl a chance, why don't you?* "Here. And, yes, I went back with her to her dormitory so I know how to find her if she doesn't show up. We also obtained permission from the doctor for the results of her tests to be phoned to us here at the casita. She said she'd prefer to come here than the hospital. Oh! And I bought her some prenatal multivitamins."

"Oh?" He pulled open a drawer and shifted things around until he unearthed a small yellow pad. "I can get you a reimbursement right away."

Harriet waved it away with a smile. "This one can be on me. I have a daily stipend from St. Nick's and since I haven't been out at all since I arrived it's not a problem."

"Were you planning on doing much sightseeing?" Matteo leaned back in his chair, an eyebrow quirked with curiosity.

Harriet stayed silent, fighting the urge to scream. Or cry. She'd fought that urge frequently over the past few days. She obviously knew him less well than she'd thought, but, goodness gracious, Matteo really knew how to bring out the heavily ignored ends of her emotional spectrum.

The sting of tears threatened as her fingers crept up to give her locket a rub. *C'mon Harriet! You're the calm, rational, steady-tempered twin.* And yet she was already beginning to feel worn, careening from one emotional extreme to the other. This was all new terrain for her and if Matteo would just take a few moments to behave with a bit of much-needed *compassion*, it would be much easier to approach the next few weeks with Mr. Grumpy with a smile.

"No," Harriet amazed herself by replying in a bright voice. "As I said on the first day, I am here to work. So, if you'll excuse me...?" She didn't even wait for a reply, just turned on her heel and swiftly left the clinic.

She needed to get to her tiny little room, and fast. Its cozy interior had given her comfort in the past few days as she'd adjusted to the new surroundings, the new language, the new Matteo.

Miraculously, she managed to maintain the tiniest grip of emotional control until she reached her room. The last thing she was going to do was let Matteo see her cry. Let him know how much she longed to be with him. Because that was what was happening. She was fighting desire the way a musketeer fought baddies. With every ounce of energy she had.

Harriet shut the door to her room behind her, only just making it to her bed before the tears began to flow in earnest. It was all she could do to stop the sobs burning her chest from filling the room. She stuffed her head into her pillow and poured the tumult of emotions into the downy silencer. She cried until there were no more tears. Her emotions spent, she rolled onto her back and stared into the growing darkness of her room.

They worked well together, her ever rational side told her. And that's what she needed to focus on. All the emotional tension bouncing between them had stood in the way of her really putting her nose to the grindstone for the assessment she'd promised Dr. Bailey.

She pushed herself up in surprise.

She hadn't thought of Dr. Bailey or St. Nick's, not really, for...*days*. A whole week! The world she had thought completed her own had all but disappeared since she had been here. It didn't take much divining to know it was a "who" rather than a "what" that had opened her eyes to so much more in the world.

She lay back on to the quilt with a heightened sense of awareness of just how much she had seen and learned in such a short time.

Her mind drifted and wandered and she realized with a start she must've dozed off as her room was cloaked in darkness. The night was still warm and her small window was cracked open enough to smell the fresh scent of the late-night air. She'd have to be fully awake in a few hours, ready for a new day. A day where she and Matteo would behave with professional respect towards each other and nothing more. Just as the Queen herself might've behaved.

An ironic smile hit her lips in gratitude for her English stoicism. Her ability to behave as if everything was perfectly all right, even if everything inside her was devastated by a romance that could never be.

She stood to undo her blouse and skirt, uncharacteristically letting them drop to the floor. She lay back on the bed, focusing on the sensation of the well-worn cotton sheet against her skin. The softness of it. She shifted a leg, imagining the soft caress of the sheet was, in fact, Matteo's hands. His fingers skimming along the length of her thigh. A warmth began to grown within her. She knew she should fight it, but didn't. Just this once.

Her hands shifted across her belly. She was surprised to feel how soft it was. The tiniest of arcs upwards, instead of the gentle slope and swoop it normally made. She hadn't remembered eating more than she usually did. Sure, the food here was good but… She laid her hands on top of her belly as if it would help her divine if her body really had changed or if she was imagining things.

A thought came to her. A shocking thought.

She lifted her hands and moved them so that they hovered above her breasts. When she finally raised the courage to touch them, feeling the added plumpness, recalling the slight hint of blue veins she had noted but dismissed that morning, she knew instantly what she needed to do. Inching herself out of bed as if she were surrounded by a floor full of sleeping children, she moved with exaggerated stealth. After tugging on a T-shirt and her skirt, she decided to forego flip-flops and, as quietly as she could, made her way to the clinic.

By the time she arrived, her stomach was churning. She clicked the door shut as quietly as she could, hoping the light wouldn't disturb anyone in the courtyard. She checked the wall clock. Three a.m.

All being well, she would have the place to herself for a while.

Good. She would need the privacy for what she was about to do.

She went to the cupboard to get the nail-file-length stick, sheathed in its protective foil wrapping. They preferred to let teenage girls who needed the test to use these at first. It brought them some privacy. Some time to register what might or might not be happening in their bellies.

The door to the loo gave an eerie creak as she pulled it open and scanned the room, as if the noise would suddenly bring all of the children running. She waited a few moments, just to be safe, then closed herself in the small room to take the test.

It was nearly impossible to keep up with surge after surge of thoughts and images racing through her mind as the seconds ticked past at an interminably slow pace.

Sitting in the loo wasn't helping, so she pushed out of the door and back into the clinic just as the front door opened.

"*Que paso?* What's going on?"

It was Matteo. Green eyes dark as a forest, worry lines creasing his forehead.

Harriet's heart all but stopped beating, a shiver of goose pimples shuddering down her arms as she met his beautiful eyes again.

"Harriet?"

She looked at him, the test dangling from her fingers, completely tongue-tied. She knew and she didn't. All it would take was one look.

"Harriet?" Matteo asked again, the concern in his voice growing tighter. "Is everything all right?"

She lifted the test between them, holding it so that they could both see the little window where there either would or wouldn't be a brightly colored plus sign.

Both of them stayed stationary as the result of the test registered, first visually, then cognitively, and as her body began to tremble, Harriet returned her unblinking gaze to Matteo's wide-eyed expression and spoke the words they both already knew.

"I'm pregnant."

The words rang and rang in Matteo's ears.

Words he'd thought he'd never hear in his wildest dreams.

And not just hearing. Seeing the *proof*!

Everything he'd counseled the countless teens he'd seen in the same situation completely left him. For the very first time he knew exactly how they felt. Lost. Bewildered. Hopeful. Terrified. Microseconds away from panic gripping every one of his carefully controlled sensibilities.

He pressed his lips together to stop himself from asking the questions he already knew the answers to. They had used protection. She hadn't been with anyone else. So the "mistakes happen" adage was true. It was his child. The child growing in Harriet's belly was his.

His eyes fixed on her hands, protectively crossed over her tummy, the maternal instinct already alive and well within her.

A primal urge to erase the fear racing through her eyes took hold of him but his gut checked him. And in the instant he hesitated he could see resolve harden in her eyes.

"Don't worry, I've already figured out that you don't want children."

"How?"

"I'm not blind."

"What are you talking about?"

"You keep the children at arm's length. You are kind but you certainly aren't cuddly with them."

"What does any of that prove?"

"You don't like to get close to them. I mean, what kind of pediatrician doesn't like to hold babies?"

The words struck him physically, rendering him speechless. All he could do was return her wide-eyed gaze. Had he really been that transparent?

Harriet backed away from him, her voice a steady confirmation of the decision she must've made in an instant. "I'm going back to England soon enough. In just a few weeks, maybe sooner. No one has to know."

"Harriet, we don't need to make any decisions tonight. Give me time. Time to—"

"Time to want this less than you do right now?"

She shook her head in stiff, infinitesimally smaller shakes. If he hadn't felt hyper-aware of her every movement, he might have missed them. "No one has to know. It's not your problem."

His hands clenched and released. Clenched and released. None of this was right. The last thing he wanted was for Harriet to have this moment—the moment she found out she was pregnant—feel like a problem. But he had vowed on his sister's grave never to have children. Had closed his heart to the possibility.

"Is that what you want? What you're happy with?" He could've cracked his head against the wall at the selfishness of his questions.

"It's not as if I've had much time to make sense of this! You just walked in on me."

"I thought someone was breaking into the clinic so I—"

"You thought I was a *criminal*?" She all but recoiled.

"I didn't know who it was. I just saw a figure and..." He stopped himself. Being argumentative with a woman—*the woman who was pregnant with his child*—when she'd just found out was a bad idea. A very bad idea.

"I think I'd like to go to my room."

"We can talk about this. *Mi amor.*" The words came naturally. The feelings were real. He cared for her and it surprised him to realize just how much.

She shook her head at his words, rejecting his affection. "Harriet," he corrected himself. He'd told her there was nothing between them when she'd barely disembarked from the plane and now he was proving it.

"No. We can't talk about it. I have to decide what I am going to do about my baby. Alone."

It nearly broke his heart to see her skirt round him to get to the door as if fearful that touching him would cause her pain.

He reached out to her, hoping for… Who knew what—a moment of stillness? A moment to absorb the enormity of what was happening?

Harriet pressed herself against the wall, raising her hands as she did so.

"I think it's best if I go to my room now."

Tears were glistening in her eyes. He ached to reach out, soothe them away. Tuck the little stray honey-blonde twists of hair away from her eye-line. Caress away the deep furrow tugging her brows tightly together.

She was right, of course. To back away.

The idea of being a father... He felt his lungs constrict. It was the one thing he had been certain of since his sister had died. He did not want children. He'd said it like a mantra over the years. He did not want children, and yet—

"You don't have to do this alone." As the words came out he knew they sounded pathetic. He was unconvinced so how on earth was she ever to believe him?

"Don't worry, Matteo." Harriet turned round once she'd reached the safety of the doorway, a bitter-sweet smile tipping up the edges of her lips. "You're right. I won't have to do it alone. I have my sister."

The words were like a knife in his heart. She had a sister.

Harriet couldn't know how cruel her choice of words was. And how perfect a reminder they were of why he'd vowed to never have a family of his own. How could he when he hadn't noticed his own sister's extended absences? Hadn't pinned her down, demanded an explanation, showed her the unconditional love a brother owed a sister? If he had well and truly been there for Ramona, she'd be here today. And Harriet's news could be... It would be good news.

He cursed under his breath. They'd used protection! He should've taken a cue from the monastic lodgings and practiced abstinence. He'd never imagined himself leaving a woman in the lurch, but, more pressingly, he'd vowed to never have a child. He had nothing to offer.

At least Harriet wouldn't be alone. She had family. A loving sister with newborns just a few weeks away. It would be a chaotic household but there was little doubt it would be a loving one. Her family would be there for her, comforting, supportive. There, in every way that he couldn't be. He leant against the closed door and sank to the floor, head bowed in his hands as the numbness of grief began to settle in.

CHAPTER SEVEN

HARRIET STARED AT the phone in her hand, not knowing whether to feel shell-shocked or elated. Perhaps a bit of both? What she did know was she had about a gazillion questions to ask her sister. And another gazillion she wasn't quite ready to answer.

It was fitting, she thought, that she was up to her elbows in babygrows and stacks of muslin squares when the telephone call came. After a handful of hours when she hadn't even bothered to try to sleep, she'd overheard Matteo telling the casita's matron he was going out for the entire morning on business, so she'd been folding the casita's never-ending stack of laundry in the courtyard, hoping the fresh air would help clear the chaos playing out in her mind. Apart from that, hiding in her room wasn't exactly going to make her *un*-pregnant. Pregnant with Matteo's baby. Right here, right now. And he wanted nothing to do with it. With her.

She'd just closed her eyes to take in a waft of the floral scents exuding from the arbor she'd tucked herself in to avoid the midday sun when her phone rang.

Her sister's news had come in a torrent and the phone call had ended as abruptly, leaving Harriet reeling in her hidden nook of flowers and vines. The arbor shielded her from the rush and buzz of life in the courtyard. Which was exactly what she needed right now. A bit of privacy until she knew how to respond. Which, realistically, she was not going to figure out how to do until she spoke to her sister again.

She punched the long number into the phone and waited for the foreign ringtone to sound in her ear.

"Harri!" Her sister answered before the first ring had finished sounding. "Are you all right?"

"Shouldn't I be asking you that question or jumping on a plane or practicing my double diaper changing skills?" Harriet felt the tension slip from her shoulders at the sound of her sister's laugh. She'd always derived such strength from her. Claudia's passion, drive and overall joie de vivre were unparalleled. The fact she couldn't be with her now was almost physically painful.

"Don't be silly. I told you I was in good hands."

Oh.

They'd always been there for each other. Harriet had made sure of it. But this time...did her sister not need her? She shook away the thought and forced on a sunny voice.

"I know, I know. But I think I was in a bit of shock when you told me everything. So...this time I need a blow-by-blow recap." And that was putting it mildly. Harriet was experiencing shock at news of her own pregnancy. Shock at the turn of events in her sister's life. It was a wonder she hadn't lost the plot entirely.

"Where do you want me to begin?"

Before Harriet could respond she heard her sister give a happy exclamation. "Ooh! Beea-*uuu*-tiful!"

"What?" She ached to be in Los Angeles at her sister's side, experiencing the highs and lows of life vicariously, just as she had done throughout her childhood...always a bit too painfully shy to experience her own.

"Sorry, Har! A nurse just came in and faked a faint at my flowers. My big beautiful bouquet of flowers that *he* sent."

"Who?" Harriet all but squealed.

"Dr. Spencer." Her voice softened. "Patrick."

"Patrick?" Harriet's defensive sister radar went on high alert. "Who's Patrick?"

"I told you, he's the obstetrician who was in the elevator. The lift," she corrected herself.

"Where you had the babies."

"Yes! Didn't you listen to anything I said the first time?"

"Of course I…" Harriet faltered. Of course she had—but the news was so huge and with her mind still buzzing with her own pregnancy it was all a bit overwhelming. "I'm an auntie!" Tears sprang to her eyes. A mix of elation and sorrow that her sister had had her babies but that the birth had been so fraught with danger. Six weeks early and trapped in a lift. Things only Claudia could turn into silver linings.

"Harri…is everything all right?" Claudia had always been able to read her mind, even at long distance.

"Of course. I just…" *I'm having a baby and the*

man I love doesn't want me. "I can't believe you had to go through so much."

"I must admit I'm actually grateful I wasn't conscious when everything happened with the hysterectomy. I think Patrick went through more trauma than I did—and I will be eternally grateful for what he did for me and my two little baby boys."

"Of course. He sounds—"

"Lovely," Claudia finished for her.

Hmm… Not necessarily the word Harriet would've chosen—but now she knew what her sister thought of her Doctor in Shining Armor. A double birth in a lift chased up by a hysterectomy that had ultimately saved her life. But it meant she would never have any more children. It was hard to believe her sister sounded so…so… vital! Then again, that was Claudia through and through. Vital. Brave. Undeterred. Instinctively, her hand slipped to her own belly, feeling a rush of gratitude for the microscopic life blossoming within her. You really never knew what life was going to throw at you.

This was her sister's moment, though. She would wait to tell Claudia her news another day.

"Well, I definitely owe him a thank-you card for saving my sister!"

"And you're still having the time of your life in Argentina?"

Tears began to trickle down Harriet's cheeks as she nodded. That was one way to put it.

"Harri? Are you sure you're all right?"

"Of course!" Her voice squeaked a bit as she regrouped. "I'm just so happy you're safe and the babies are safe and I just wish I could be there for you."

"Don't worry, little sis. We'll be together in London before you know it. Now!" Her sister's voice turned uncharacteristically schoolmarmy. "I know you and I am officially telling you to quit worrying about me. Go out and enjoy Buenos Aires with that hot doc of yours!"

"I never said he was hot." Harriet bridled.

"You didn't have to." Claudia laughed and then gave a sharp gasp.

"Claudy! Are you okay?" Harriet fretted, instantly forgetting her sister's instruction.

"Yes. Yes—just testing all my new stitches. Harri, everything's fine with me so just go and enjoy yourself for once! No need to worry. I'm in good hands."

Something about the way Claudia's tone shifted indicated to Harriet a certain Dr. Spencer may have just entered the room. She felt comforted and a bit bruised by the realization her sister seemed to have someone else in the role of caregiver. She'd always been the one who was there for her sister when things went topsy-turvy. Hadn't she?

"Love you, sis." Harriet swiped away a fresh whoosh of tears.

"Love you, too, little sis!"

"It was only by a minute!" Harriet wailed by rote.

"Yes. Which makes me older and wiser," Her sister retorted. "Now, go on, have a steak for me! And a dance! Tango under the stars, Harri. Make sure you live a little."

And the line clicked off.

Harriet's fingers instinctively began toying with her locket. For the last ten years it had just been the two of them. Harriet and Claudia against the world! Or, more accurately, Harriet on standby while Claudia took on the world.

Now it would be Claudia, her two little boys and maybe…a Patrick?

Was it finally time to stop living life's Big Moments through her sister? Have moments of her own? A child. A family?

Her hands slipped down to her tummy. Planned or not, she had the baby part covered. Just no Mr. Right.

An image of Matteo popped into her mind… all lean, sexy, smiley… He was Mr. Right for All the Wrong Reasons. Like it or not, she knew in her heart she was in love with him and would just have to live with the fact the love wouldn't be returned.

Her fingers traced a circle round her tummy before returning to the laundry, her hands folding on automatic pilot as she processed all the new information.

An auntie! A *mother*… Of all the things she'd never let herself imagine she would be, she was going to be a mother. The news was going to take a while to feel anything close to real, let alone something she would tell people. And by people she meant her sister.

"Someone looks happy!" Matteo called from

the courtyard, the usual stream of children following in his wake. She stared at him as if he wasn't real, only to realize he was still speaking. "If I'd known folding made you so smiley, I would have put you on laundry duty from the get-go."

Play along...just play along for now. There's time. "Yes, it's the first thing I mastered in Nursing 101." She pushed up from the blanket where she'd been sitting to a kneeling position and considered him.

Was this how they were going to deal with things? Ignore the baby elephant in the courtyard? It would be tough but, then again, they hadn't even had a day to process what was happening. Besides, she was English. Suppressing emotion in the face of adversity was her forté. Time to fly the Union Jack for baby Monticello! Or Torres. Monticello-Torres? No...that sounded pretentious. She shook her head clear and looked up with a smile as he approached.

"I've just had some very good news, actually."

"Ah! Good news! That's something we enjoy here." Matteo's smile hit her straight in the heart and did its usual warm twirly journey around her insides. There was no point in fighting it. He gave her a funny tummy. That's just how things were. But winning his heart as he had won hers? There was no chance of that happening. Zero.

"Eh, bribónes! *Vaminos."* He shooed away a gaggle of boys starting up a game of football on the edges of the arbor. "You should all be having lunch now. Make your bodies and brains grow a bit more before we get you back to school, *ai*?"

Harriet smiled. It was nice to see him with the children. He was a complete natural. Funny sometimes, serious when he needed to be. Reliable. She understood perfectly the complexities of working in an orphanage—and it warmed her to see the abundance of affection the children received here. Matteo obviously held the respect of all of them. He wasn't a cuddly presence but he was a loved one. What was it that stopped him from loving babies? Their baby? Suppress, suppress, suppress! *More time to digest...that's what we need.*

"So..." Matteo settled on a bench across from her, grabbing an armful of laundry from her pile as he did so. "What's this news?"

She opened her mouth to tell him and found

herself mimicking a goldfish. What took precedence here? The birth of her nephews? The lift? The doctor? The hysterectomy? The fact her sister didn't want her to jump on a plane was the one that hurt most. Harriet the One Woman Support Team her sister always called her. But not this time.

Her sister had *always* wanted her.

Tears popped into her eyes and she knew if she spoke, they'd start cascading down her cheeks.

Uh-oh. Too late. No speaking required.

"Hey." Matteo was kneeling beside her before she had a moment to understand what was happening, the back of his hand wiping away the freshly spilt tears. She batted his hand away. Feeling his touch was too close to affection. Something she didn't want to get used to.

"It's my sister," she managed, surges of emotion tightening her throat.

"What's happened?" He was all alertness now, ready for action. Despite herself, she smiled through her tears, a hiccough working its way to the surface before she managed to speak. She felt about six years old—a first! And her untamable sister was a mother!

She looked at Matteo, knowing that if he was only willing, there were a thousand possibilities lying right there within his arms. But allowing herself to dream would only lead to more heartbreak. She sucked in a breath and refocused. This was about her sister. Not about a romance that was never going to happen.

"She's had her twins."

"*Amor!* That's wonderful. Congratulations to you all." Before she knew what was happening, Matteo's cheek was on hers, kisses being planted on first one side of her face then the other, lips shifting past hers in a happy blur of scent and sensation. She became aware of his hands holding her shoulders first close to him then further back so that he could inspect her.

"So these are happy tears, yes?"

"Of course, yes," she replied, swiping at her wet cheeks, masking her face with her fingers so she could regroup. "It's just…"

She felt him watching her expectantly, looking so *vital* as he waited for information. He wasn't to be her lover. Or a father to their child. Was she ever going to learn to be near him and not ache for more?

Despite a very early morning email to St. Nick's insisting she already knew Casita Verde fitted the criteria for a new clinic, Dr. Bailey had insisted she stay the agreed duration. Told her it would be good for her. Torture was more like it!

She really needed a friend right now and her choices were startlingly limited. She peeked at Matteo through her fingers. Could she shore up her emotional reserves to face a friendship with him with no promise of love? Maybe if she'd been some sort of elegant film star from the nineteen-thirties…or a rock star…or… Harriet Monticello, Nurse At Large?

Matteo sat next to her, patiently waiting for her to collect herself, pulling one of her hands into his, a thumb idly stroking across the back of her hand. She kept her eyes on his thumb shifting this way and that as she made her decision.

"It wasn't an easy birth," she began. Then the story poured out. The dramatic birth in the elevator, the emergency services, the doctor who had miraculously been in the lift with her at the time, the hysterectomy that had followed.

"It must've been difficult for her, to have had that decision made on her behalf."

"Yes. I can't imagine not having any control over whether or not I had children." The words were out before she'd thought them through.

Matteo placed her hand back in her lap and began to pluck away the petals of a fallen flower, discarding them one by one as if they were thoughts he was no longer interested in. "It sounds as though it's all turned out well, though?"

Harriet dipped her head, swatting at a stray tear. "Yes, that's true. She's got the twins, healthy and sound. So it's not as if she has no children. And she has me," she added, trying to add a bit of chirpiness to her tone. "I told her I'd jump on a plane tonight."

"Oh?"

It was difficult to tell what meaning his tight response held.

"You'd want to be with your sister if she'd just had a baby, wouldn't you?"

It came out defensively. And was meant to have been hypothetical. But she knew in an instant she'd hit on something much closer to home, something deeply, deeply painful.

She started to form an apology but didn't know

how. She didn't know what she'd be apologizing for.

"She is very lucky. To have a sister as dedicated as you are." Matteo smoothed past the fractured moment with a cursory pat on her knee. One you'd distractedly give to a child who'd just found out they'd done well on an inconsequential exam.

What's hurt you so badly? Is it why you want nothing to do with me? With our child?

"Well, I agree," Harriet shot back, injecting a bit of righteous indignation into her voice. Feeling the need to keep up the facade that something hadn't just happened. "But that's the part..." Her voice caught in her throat again. She couldn't believe how hard it was to say the words.

"Harriet." Matteo's brow furrowed with concern. "What is it?"

"Oh, blimey—it's almost ridiculous! I'm behaving like a child, but..." She all but choked the words out. "She said I shouldn't come."

"What?" Matteo's eyebrows shot up, indignant on her behalf. "Is she not grateful to have a sister so concerned?"

Harriet waved away the shock of his response.

"No, no. I didn't mean it like that. Of course

she wants me to meet the babies and things, but she said not to come right away, she's being taken care of. She knows I've only got a few weeks here and she was planning to come to London anyway. You know, once I'm done here. It's just weird not to be helping. It's…um… It's…" She blew a steadying breath between her lips, unsuccessfully stemming the flow of more tears. "It's what I've always done! Been there for her. I've always been the one she could rely on!" The words flew out as a plaintive cry, but were very heartfelt. If she hadn't been feeling so overwhelmed by everything, she'd be feeling like a Class-A idiot. Crying like a child because things weren't going The Way They Always Had.

C'mon, Harriet! She wants you to live your own life. Not in the shadows of hers.

"Of course you want to be with her. It's only natural."

Matteo pushed himself up from the ground where he'd been kneeling beside Harriet, sitting well back on the deep bench, elbows dug into his knees, hands holding his chin in support as he thought how to respond. He couldn't bear seeing Harriet cry, but was in no position to make decisions for her. He'd all but denied paternity of their child—and was humbled she was speaking to him at all.

He forced himself to focus on the immediate scenario. If Claudia had been his sister he would've been on a plane in an instant. But that choice was not—and never would be—available to him.

"Your sister is your only family, *sí*?"

Harriet nodded, accepting the handkerchief Matteo tugged out of his pocket, twisting it back and forth in her hands after she'd dabbed at her nose and eyes.

"If you want to go, you must go. Family is paramount." He all but flinched at his own words. He could have a family if he wanted. With Harriet. Yet he'd made it clear it wasn't an option. *Was choosing a life alone really the answer?*

"But she's the one telling me not to come!" Harriet reminded him.

"Is her health in danger?"

"No, no." Harriet gave a tiny shake of her head. "She's in good hands. Receiving excellent medical care. I'm sure of that. It's just—it's not so easy as just hopping on a plane."

"Sure it is. My parents go back and forth to America all the time. They have a company jet. If you need to go, you will go with them. Just say the word."

Matteo tried to keep his expression neutral. He wasn't in the habit of offering rides on his parents' private jet, but this was important. Even they would see that. A stab of guilt accompanied his thoughts. He hadn't rung them in a while. Too long. Perhaps it was time to practice what he preached a bit more proactively. Try to heal the wounds that were smarting like hell right now.

"I didn't mean like that—the logistics." Harriet stuffed his handkerchief into her pocket, making no acknowledgement of what he'd just said about his parents, and began briskly folding the clothes, as if the quick motions would help her thoughts collect and reshape into the best solution.

"Then what do you mean?"

"I mean… Ooh!" She released a cry of exasperation. "Unless you've been a twin to the most amazing sister in the world you just wouldn't understand!"

"Why, Harriet Monticello! I thought you said your sister was the dramatic one." *Risky tactic, but...ah...there's the light in her eyes I love so much.*

"I think she's trying to tell me something by saying I shouldn't come straight away. In fact, I *know* she's trying to tell me something." She gave a short, self-effacing laugh. "Mostly because she said as much. Claudia was never really one to mince words."

"She wouldn't be the older twin by any chance?" Matteo smiled, pleased to be building a more complete picture of who Harriet was. How she ticked.

"Only by one teensy-weensy minute and she never—and I mean *never*—lets me forget it!"

"So why does your older, *wiser*..." he tucked the word into air quotes "...sister think you should hold off coming to see your brand-new nephews?"

He leaned back against the thick wooden beam of the arbor, trying to give her the time, and the space, to think. Regroup. Something he should no doubt be doing himself, but ignoring everything was working pretty well for him so he was going to go with it. He put everything she'd said into order and considered...

Harriet and her twin sounded like chalk and cheese. The portrait she'd painted of Claudia conjured up a woman who never took no for an answer, who ate life up with an insatiable relish. And Harriet? She embodied kindness. Was the definition of gentleness. *Heart.* That was more like it. She was one hundred percent heart. And if he wasn't careful, she could so easily work her way into his.

A smile tugged at his lips as she yanked item after item off the diminishing pile of unfolded laundry and whipped it into shape. Her mind was obviously reeling with putting things in the right order—the emotions she was experiencing playing out on her face as she did. First a smile, collapsing into a frown, chased up by a lifted brow and lips pressed together to shift this way and that as if tasting the air for the hint of a solution.

He was willing to wait all day if that's what it took.

Que? When did that seismic shift occur?

Matteo considered Harriet through narrowed eyes—eyebrows rising as he realized how much he had changed since her arrival. He was drawn to her. Kept seeking her out "just to make sure everything was all right." Right now his time would be much better spent filling out grant applications, updating records or looking for future sites, and yet here he was, sitting in a flowery arbor wanting nothing more than to ensure she was all right. Wanting her happiness over his own. And yet he let her believe he wanted nothing to do with her—their child. What kind of man did that?

"It isn't that she doesn't want me there. In Los Angeles," Harriet finally began, a small shake left in her voice, though the tears had now dried. "Like I said, we're all organized to meet up in London at our house, the house our parents raised us in, in a few weeks anyway."

"Then what is it?"

"It's that…it's that she doesn't *need* me." Her face tightened to fight another round of tears. "She said she wants me to be happy—but I *am* happy when she needs me!"

Matteo fought an urge to lift her up from the ground and into his arms, hold her, soothe away the tears. But this was her battle and something told him to stay where he was. Let her work through the emotional turbulence on her own. What she was processing now seemed to be getting to the heart of who Harriet thought she was.

"So, let me get this straight. Your sister doesn't want you to go to Los Angeles so you will be happy—but you won't be happy unless she needs you?"

"It sounds ridiculous when you put it like that but, yes." She tossed him a guilty-as-charged expression.

Had she said something to her sister indicating she was happy here? With him?

"Do you think being needed is the same as being loved?"

"Of course not. It's just… I guess it's just always felt like *proof* that I'm worthy of being loved."

"Of course you're worthy of being loved! You're one of the most loveable people I've ever met!" They stared at one another, shell-shocked, his words hanging between them. In that moment he felt that if anyone *needed* Harriet in their lives it was him. If anyone loved Harriet it was him. He loved her, but until he laid the ghosts of the past to rest, he couldn't give her the love she deserved.

He cleared his throat, forcing the clinician in him to step in. The one who took an emotional step back from everything. From everyone.

"Have you told her you're unhappy here?"

"No."

Nice to know he hadn't been that much of an ogre.

"And how well does your sister know you?"

"Better than anyone."

"So she would know what was right…for you." He was treading on thin ice now. This was about what was best for Harriet, not about keeping her here. Even though—*¡qué diablos!*—God help him, it was what he wanted.

Harriet tipped her head back and forth, carefully considering his question. "Claudia knows how to live life."

"And you?"

"I know how to care for the living." She shot him a horrified look. "That sounds *awful*! I mean, not the caring part—I love the caring part—but it sounds like…like I'm not living."

Bingo. This, he suspected, was what Harriet's twin wanted for her. To live her own life. Not in the shadows of everyone else's.

"So…what do you want to do?" he asked cautiously.

"To live?"

Matteo couldn't help but laugh. "Are you asking me or telling me?"

"Telling? Telling." She steadied her voice and tried it again. Deeper. "Telling you." Then like a robot, "I. Am. Telling. You. I. Want. To Live."

He watched, delighted as she dissolved into laughter with another rush of tears. Tears, he was relatively sure, that were happier this time. He felt touched. Deeply so. Had he just witnessed an epiphany? Now to just sweep all of the other emotional revelations back under the carpet. He put on his officious voice.

"It sounds to me as if your sister is being well looked after. Are we agreed on that?"

"Yes." Snuffle. Giggle.

He handed over a fresh handkerchief. In his line of work, at least two were needed per day.

"And Claudia loves you very much."

"I like the way you say her name properly." Harriet blew her nose. "No one pronounces it correctly."

He laughed. He loved the way she found pleasure in the little things. Was still in her sister's corner, no matter how minor the infraction.

"Could it be that Claudia finally sees you doing something for yourself and doesn't want to be the one to bring it to an end?"

Harriet looked at him blankly, lifting her hands in an I-don't-know-what-you're-talking-about gesture.

"How often have you been there for your sister?"

"Always," she answered instantly.

"And how often do you put yourself—your needs, your desires—ahead of hers?"

Harriet shrugged uncomfortably. The answer was obviously "Never" and it wasn't sitting well.

"Is being here the first time you've done something for yourself? Stepped outside your role at the hospital: Reliable Harriet?"

"Working at St. Nick's makes me happy." Harriet responded defensively.

"Of course! I'm not saying it doesn't. But there's something in you—isn't there, *amorcita*?—wanting to break free of the role you've cast yourself in. See more. *Be* more."

"I didn't cast myself in the role! My family needed…" She stopped. Reconsidered, eyes widening as she looked at her past from a different perspective. "It was me, wasn't it? I put myself in that role. They loved me no matter what."

"*Exacto*. I would wager anything you were always loved. No matter what." The vision of a family came to Matteo. Himself, a wife, children—he wasn't sure how many—all of them laughing together as they shared a meal.

He cleared his throat again, giving his chin a rough scrub as he did so.

"Or maybe I am talking complete and utter nonsense." He filled in the growing silence between them.

"Actually…" Harriet drew out the word before conceding with a sheepish smile, "I think you might be right."

Matteo looked at her, his mind temporarily confusing the vision he'd just had with the reality. They were talking about Harriet and her sister, not some fantasy family scenario that could never exist. *Focus. Regroup.*

"My sister does want this for me. She was over the moon when she heard about you." Her eyes popped wide open, cheeks instantly going pink with embarrassment. "I mean, that I was working here."

"And what about you?" Matteo asked, his voice smokier than usual. "Do you want to stay?"

Harriet forced herself to meet the gaze she knew was resting on her, half hoping there would be an answer waiting there. They weren't talking about her sister any longer.

She knew what her heart was saying. *With every pore in my body!* But if staying meant stomping her heart into smithereens every single day…she wasn't sure how much she could take. Decisions she made for herself were now decisions she was making for her baby.

She looked into Matteo's richly hued eyes and saw kindness there. *Friendship.* But no commitment. He'd never promised it and something within her knew he was a man who stuck to his word.

The heart, thumping against her breastbone,

was telling her what she already knew. She was in love with him and would have his child.

Her brain shrank to the size of a pea then had its own Big Bang, exploding into countless trains of thought.

Was the whole situation flawed? If that meant Matteo didn't sweep her up, race hand in hand to the judge to make her his wife the moment they'd seen the pregnancy test, sure. But who did that? He was probably still in shock at the news. She knew she was. And a shotgun wedding wasn't what she wanted anyway.

She wanted to marry someone who was in love with her. And in love with babies. All babies. *Their* babies. Matteo, painfully gorgeous and kind as he was, wasn't that man. So. Home it was. Home alone.

She looked away, busying herself with some unnecessary color-coding of the laundry pile. She didn't want her child to think she was a wimp. High-tailing it home to her safe and secure life at the first sign of trouble? Okay…it was a pretty big thing, but it wasn't trouble. It was…a curve-ball. And there were pluses to staying here. She'd learn more about Matteo. Have more of a fleshed-out portrait to paint for their child one day. Understand what made the idea of having a child so inconceivable to him.

So. She'd focus on the good.

Where would she start? With those lush green eyes she could quite happily ogle until the end of time. And who had hair so beautifully *desirable*? She'd find another way to describe to her baby about the thick black hair she'd thrilled in running—no, *raking*—her fingers through in a moment of unbelievably heated passion. The night of mutual desire they'd shared had been more than she would ever have hoped for even a few weeks ago. And a surprise baby to boot? Life was certainly giving her a triple whammy in the Big Changes department. And she was going to meet them with a smile.

Matteo may not share her feelings but she knew she had it in her heart to admire him for all the things he was. Strong. Impassioned. Driven.

All traits she admired. Ones she would love for the child growing in her belly to possess. So. It was time to choose.

Need. Want. Love.

Letting go of what she'd thought life had in store for her...embracing what she did have?

The words raced around her mind as she worked her gaze round the courtyard. Not even here a fortnight and she was already enjoying the volume of hands-on work her day involved. Being a research nurse was wonderful, but it was watching, observing, noting.

Here, with the absence of resources of St. Nick's, there was little choice but to muck in and she was loving it. From laundry to nursing poorly children to helping pregnant teens give birth. It was like tapping into a side of herself she hadn't seen for a long time—if ever.

Colors seemed brighter. New aromas took her by surprise every day. The lush green and tropical citrusy scent of so many plants bursting to life, despite the fact it was winter. A very balmy version of winter it would be all too easy to get used to, she thought, shivering away the memory of a murky London in winter.

If she stayed for the few weeks she'd scheduled, she could channel her passions towards being the woman she wanted to be for her family. Her growing family.

A smile teased at her lips as she gave the final pile of folded laundry a decisive pat. She heaved up the overloaded wicker basket and shot Matteo a grateful smile.

"Thank you. You've been a great friend."

"I've not done anything." He looked bewildered.

"Of course you have!" *You've helped me to believe in me.*

"Am I missing something? Are we booking you on the next flight to America or…?"

"You're stuck with me for the time being, I'm afraid. If that's all right."

"Of course! You're welcome, for as long as you like." He reached out as if to touch her, then pulled back, stuffing his hands into his pockets. "Are you absolutely sure?"

"Yes. Pretty sure." *No.* "Definitely sure." She twisted back and forth, the laundry basket a buffer between them. "On one condition."

"Which is?"

"You treat me the same as any other staffer here." Her chin jutted out a bit, a visual confirmation that her mind was made up. She would do this thing—and do it with style.

"I will do my best." He nodded his head as he spoke.

"It's all any of us can do." And she meant it.

CHAPTER EIGHT

"Sorry to interrupt." Harriet had already tapped on Matteo's door a couple of times, to no avail, but having peeked through the open sliver of doorway she could see he was deep in thought over a pile of paperwork.

"Sì?" Worry lines creased his forehead.

"Everything all right?"

"Yes, sorry. Just…" He pushed the papers back and stood up from the desk, taking what looked to be a long overdue stretch. "Managing budgets is never much fun.

"No." Harriet gave a sympathetic smile. "That was definitely my least favorite part of the job."

"Was?"

"Is." She laughed nervously. Of course her job back at St. Nick's was still hers. Is. *Is.* "I've obviously taken to fewer responsibilities a bit too easily."

"Are you saying working here is easy?" Matteo gave her the first genuine smile she'd had from him in weeks and… Yes. It still worked. Still made her feel all gooey inside.

She leant against the door frame for a bit of support and smiled back. They'd been flat out for the past fortnight. Births, a couple of emergency Caesareans, infants needing admittance to NICU, not to mention day-to-day care of the older children. And she was getting the impression this was normal. She'd become adept at filling in anywhere there were holes in the staff roster—shifting from art lessons with the little ones who weren't yet in school, to infant care, to cooking breakfast, lunch and dinner, and on to the clinic to for pregnancy checks, scraped knees, blood tests… It had been quite a learning curve and she'd been loving every second of it. Not to mention it gave her a really thorough look at how Casita Verde worked.

The moments with Matteo? Few and far between. She afforded herself a quick scan of the room. Matteo's Inner Sanctum. People either didn't go near it or hovered outside the doorway and waited. A time limit had pressed her to go ahead and knock. It wasn't like he was scary or anything. He was just… Matteo, the casita's Lone Ranger. And his room was… Wow, it was stark. Monk-like. She'd hardly imagined him hiding away in a sultan's lair, but she hadn't expected bare walls and a single bed. Hadn't he mentioned parents? Ones who flew around the world in private planes?

"So…what can I do for you?" He was distracted. She was taking up his time.

"Oh! Yes, sorry." She pushed herself back upright and gave her blouse an unnecessary swipe. "Some of the schoolchildren are going to the zoo today and they need chaperones. I was wondering if you minded if I went along."

He stared at her blankly.

"You want to go to the zoo?"

"Well, I wouldn't say it was number one on my tourist destination list, but I haven't seen much of Buenos Aires and thought it would be a great way to be with the children and see a bit of your beautiful city."

"And you are going to the zoo?"

"Um…" She chewed on her lip for a second. *Did he have something against the zoo?* "If that's all right. They've got *capybaras* and you can feed them!" His eyes widened. *Perhaps that was a bit too enthusiastic.* He was, after all, trying to work.

"The rodents. The large ones," she explained. Another blank look. "You know, I don't have to go. There's plenty to do here." She looked over her shoulder for an invisible to-do list.

"So you don't want to go."

Was he confused or just choosing to be obtuse? Come to think of it, he looked a little...vacant. Had he even heard anything she'd said?

"Matteo." Harriet chose her words cautiously. "You look a bit funny." Okay. Maybe not that carefully.

"What?" He managed to get some ink on his cheek in examining himself for "funniness". She itched to swab it off with her thumb, give his lips a little kiss.

No! No she did not. Being pregnant with his child did not mean she automatically got kissing rights. They'd agreed to be friends. No benefits. It was sensible.

But being sensible didn't seem to have seeped through to Harriet's body, which still ached for him. Honestly? It was difficult to believe she would ever desire someone as much as—

"Sorry, I've just had my head down in the books and all I'm seeing is numbers, numbers, numbers, blurring together in a big mess." Matteo threw his hands up into the air in frustration. "Each of the numbers means a child does or does not get help, receive medicine, have new books to read…" He stopped, gave her a self-effacing look and smiled. "I'm doing it again, aren't I?"

"What?" She'd actually just been watching his beautiful lips move. She'd heard this speech before. Not that he was boring. Not by a long shot.

"Telling you what you already know."

There was that smile again. My goodness, the man had one heck of a bobby dazzler.

"Matteo…"

"Yes, Harriet?" He pronounced her name formally as if they'd suddenly been transported to Edwardian times. It made her laugh. Relax. He was good at that, too.

"Do you fancy coming to the zoo with me?"

"How many buckets of feed do you think we have gone through already?"

"I don't know. Maybe three? I'm sure the children have had loads more!" Harriet squinted up at him, shielding her eyes from the sun.

"The children have had two—I don't think they'll be wanting another now that they're all mesmerized by the bears, the little savages. Quit dodging, Miss Monticello. How many buckets of feed have you gone through?" Matteo didn't really care. It was just fun to quiz her. She had more of her sister in her than she'd thought. Harriet didn't do anything by halves and feeding the free-roaming animals at the zoo was no different. A genuine carer, no matter what the species. Their child would be well loved. He bit down hard on the inside of his cheek, forcing himself to focus on her reply.

"Uh…let me see. The first bucket was when we saw the baby deer…"

Matteo watched avidly as she added a finger to her bottom lip each time she counted a new bucket. Had he realized how beautiful her mouth was when he'd first seen her in London? Stupid question. Of course he had. Otherwise he wouldn't have… It was meant to be one night! And yet—hadn't he been the one to convince her to stay when her sister had her twins? A twin having twins. His eyes slipped to Harriet's belly. Could she be having...?

"Four?" Her lips parted into an I-don't-know-how-it-happened expression and he couldn't help but laugh. A little bit of panic was in there. Quadruplets? *Híjole!* Then he'd really have to step up.

He swallowed.

Like he was now? At arm's length and promising nothing?

"Four isn't that many buckets of feed, is it?"

Feed. Yes. Of course. They were talking about feed. Plenty of time to confront his demons in the midnight hours.

"There's more kid in you than in some of these kids!" he teased, hoping she'd missed his mini panic attack and had seen instead the hit of genuine gratitude he felt at being invited along. The day had been fun. She was the only person who'd managed to bring out the funster in him. The man he hadn't tapped into since his sister had died. It hadn't seemed right. It hadn't seemed fair.

"Well, it's been ages since I've been to the zoo and you can't feed the animals like this in London. Such lovely, furry, furry little beasts! It's good therapy!"

Matteo rolled his eyes good-naturedly. A few weeks ago he would've rolled his eyes and walked away. Who was he kidding? A few weeks ago you wouldn't have found him wandering round the zoo.

"Is this your covert way of saying I need fixing?"

"Don't worry—I'm the last person who is going to try and fix you!" Her eyes widened, fingers flying to cover her mouth in horror.

Without even thinking, Matteo slung an arm over her shoulder and squeezed her in for a little cuddle. She hadn't meant anything by it. No point in feeling bad.

"*Ai*, you make me laugh, *amorcita*. Not many people are brave enough to speak the truth." He dropped a kiss on her forehead as if he did it all the time. *Wanted to do all the time?*

"It's not normally what I do, either!" She looked up into his eyes, cheeks going pink at the connection. "I guess…you bring out the bravery in me."

He could have pulled her into his arms right there and then, kissed her and kissed her until the rest of the world just faded away. Her soft blonde hair was a fluff of gentle waves, her blue eyes so clear and true. He was already halfway there, holding her tucked under his arm like a delicate, beautiful bird, her chin tilted up towards his face, her eyes asking questions neither of them dared to voice. He felt another deep hit of emotion. *Love?* Had he reached a point where he felt his sister's death had been…been what? Avenged? That didn't sit right. Would sharing his fears with Harriet help her understand? His head bent just a touch closer to hers, his lips parting as he moved. She blinked, but didn't pull away. *Could he give her everything she deserved?*

"There they are!"

Matteo looked swiftly to his right to see a clutch of children on high-speed approach. He and Harriet, it appeared, were the endgame of a pell-mell race to the finish line. They split apart instantly, moved by a gut instinct not to be seen holding one another like lovers, or to be barreled down by racing children.

The littlest of the boys, Tico, emerged from the scramble of children, his face triumphant with near success. They were only a few meters away and against all odds he was pulling ahead of the taller children. Tico was going to win!

"Oh, no!"

Harriet saw it coming at the same time Matteo did. One foot tangled with the other and just short of reaching his goal Tico's small body became airborne, crashing into Harriet's—both of them landing on the ground with a *thunk*. When Tico raised his head, blood flowed from his mouth as if he had an endless supply. Matteo didn't know whether to check Tico or Harriet first. The baby. Was the baby all right?

Harriet met his frantic expression, hand on her stomach, and nodded. *Everything was fine.* She and the baby were fine.

"Me gano?" Tico asked, adrenaline from the race still pumping through him. Victory was more important than the pain he would soon be feeling.

"Did you win?" asked Harriet, trying not to look aghast at the boy's bloodied face. "What was the finish line?"

"You!"

"In that case..." she smiled, pulling some clean tissues from her shoulder bag "...you are definitely the winner!"

"¡Gane!" Tico pushed his hands to the ground

to press himself up but instantly yanked his wrist to his chest as if it had been bitten.

"May I see?" Matteo reached out, gently laying out the boy's small wrist across his hand. Swelling had already begun to inflate the area between his hand and his arm. "Looks like you might need a trip to the hospital." He looked up at the other children gathering round to gawp at Tico and his injuries. "We need to get you back to school as well, eh?"

"I'll take him," Harriet volunteered, already making short work of the blood around Tico's mouth in an effort to find the source of the bleeding.

"No! The hospitals here are zoos!" *Ha!* The irony of it all. More pressingly, a pregnant woman in endless queues surrounded by people who had who knew what? It wasn't worth it. Not at this stage in her pregnancy.

If they had their own clinic, they wouldn't be at the mercy of the long wait that would no doubt greet them at A and E. Even having an X-ray machine would make a world of difference. And there it was again—the center point of his conundrum. Being with Harriet, loving her, loving their child would all detract from the undivided attention he needed to have to make the casita a success.

He laid Tico's hand back across the boy's chest, just above his heart, and folded the boy's other arm up to hold it.

"I'll go, Harriet."

"Tico, can you give me a smile?" Harriet continued, her focus on the little boy absolute.

"Why?" he asked before complying. A big, bloody gap was immediately visible. A gap that hadn't been there a minute earlier.

Harriet—in true form—didn't flinch. She just smiled, gave the boy's cheek a stroke with the backs of her fingers. Matteo chided himself. Of course! Her concern was for the boy. His own was for a lofty aspiration that in reality would most likely never be realized.

"You haven't got your big-boy teeth yet, have you?" Harriet asked.

"No. Why?" Tico worked his tongue up to the front of his mouth and quickly realized he was missing his two front teeth. Big brown eyes widened before tears came—fear and pain suddenly overwhelming his joy at winning the race.

"May I have a closer look?"

Matteo pressed himself up to standing as Harriet checked to see whether or not the roots of the teeth had gone. Harriet was doing a good job and obviously didn't need his help. Feeling a bit of a spare part, he called to the other children to once again make more room. As the pain kicked in, there would no doubt be more tears. Tears the little boy would most likely rather shed while being held in the comfort of Harriet's arms.

Matteo's hands balled into fists of pure frustration. He could do with a spell in those arms as well. Had one night with Harriet all but undone ten years of discipline? His entire adult life he'd been able separate physical attraction from his emotions. With Harriet they were becoming so interwoven it was almost impossible to separate them. She wasn't due to stay much longer. The time had raced by. He could do this. He had to do it. For the countless teens and children who needed his help.

"All right, kids. Shall we go and find the rest of your class?"

He ignored the chorus of "No!" and *"Por favor!"* he received at his rhetorical question and began to corral them, away from Tico and Harriet. All children loved gawping at a good injury. Lucky they didn't know what was happening inside his chest right now. He'd have a dozen pairs of eyes on him.

He scribbled out the name and address of the hospital Harriet should go to, promising to call a resident he knew there. "Maybe he'll be able to bump you up the queue."

She shot him a dubious look. Even he knew his hopeful face hadn't looked too positive.

"It's all right. We'll be fine." She helped Tico up to his feet, his eyes still glued to the dirt path in a vain attempt to find his missing teeth. "Perhaps—" she lowered her voice "—the children could have a look for..." She pointed at her own front teeth. "Just in case."

"Of course, *mija*. Anything." Their eyes met again, cinched by the link of so much more than the words they spoke.

She shook her head and looked away. He'd overstepped the mark. Pushing her away, pulling her close again. His intentions were in the right place, but in practice they were verging on cruel.

"Come on, Tico. Let's see what's happening inside that wrist of yours."

She looked over her shoulder as she left, a smile only just visible on her lips. It was for him. To comfort him.

Selfless. Courageous. In a league of her own. He knew who the better of the pair of them was, and yet he was letting her walk away, taking their child with her.

CHAPTER NINE

"WHAT DID THE orthopedist say?"

Matteo held open Casita Verde's thick wooden door for Harriet and her seven-year-old charge. They'd been gone for hours. Enough time for him to regroup. Be friendly. Professional. Just what they'd agreed their relationship was. Professional.

Then again, meet and greet wasn't usually part of the "professional" service. And "usually" had all but gone out the window since Harriet had arrived. Perhaps a bit more regrouping was in order.

"As you thought…" Harriet ruffled the little boy's head "…it turns out wild races to reach the finish line first sometimes result in a wrist fracture. Not to mention losing your front teeth and gaining a unicorn horn!" The boy gave a gap-toothed grin, a huge lump already coloring the center of his forehead. "You're young— aren't you?" Harriet addressed the lad as if they'd known each other for years. "As soon as your grown-up teeth come along, you'll be as right as rain."

"I didn't mean to trip." The little boy sighed dramatically.

"Of course not, *chiquito*. It was a rather spectacular win. I'm sure the other children were incredibly impressed!" She switched to Spanish to rattle off a list of things he'd have to do to make sure his arm healed quickly. Well, not exactly *rattle*.

Matteo fought a smile as she spoke. In just a few weeks her speech had morphed into an amalgam of her native tongue and his. A lilting Spanglish. It never failed to light up his heart to see the children explaining things to her in Spanish, only to have her reply in English, the children nodding along as if it were the most normal way in the world to communicate. He couldn't quibble. It obviously worked. Who knew a stint of "orphan immersion" could be so effective a language tool? Perhaps he should run courses.

"I'll just take Tico up to his room as it's well past his bedtime and then maybe we can go over some of the children's charts?" Harriet asked, stifling a yawn.

"Absolutely, if it doesn't put you to sleep."

"No!" she protested, embarrassed he'd caught her. "Sorry. I'm sparko every afternoon and I missed out on my siesta today."

"Sparko?"

"British slang for out like a light," she explained.

"Out like a light?" asked Tico, his little face raised to the adults' in consternation.

"*Dormido.* Asleep," Harriet clarified with a grin, another yawn working its way to the surface.

"*Vamonos.* I'll get some *mate* going in the kitchen to help you stay awake!" Matteo thought for a moment. *Yerba mate* flowed in the blood of nearly all Argentinians but it had caffeine in it, something Harriet needed to be careful of in her pregnancy. Maybe mint tea would be better.

He paused, watching her lead the gangly boy away, her arm protectively wrapped across his thin shoulders. He liked seeing her blonde head tilted towards Tico's jet-black hair, a smile lighting up his face as she whispered something that made the boy giggle.

A natural comforter.

She'll be an incredible mother.

The thought came with an unexpected sting of jealousy. If—*when*—she left she would no doubt move on. Could even fall in love with another man. The thought of someone else by Harriet's side, helping to raise his child, having a family of their own didn't sit well. Not at all.

He raked a hand through his hair with a huff of impatience and headed towards the clinic. He was letting himself care too much. Feel too much. Harriet wasn't a permanent fixture. She was here to help secure funding for a proper medical center. Four weeks. That was it.

What they had shared in London?

Best to put all of those thoughts back into the further recesses of his mind and forget about them. Some things were simply not meant to be. Even if his heart kept telling him otherwise.

He pushed open the door to the clinic and was assaulted by a riot of color. Another splash of Harriet.

"You couldn't make do with plain old black and white, could you?

"Not my choice." Harriet entered the clinic behind him, arms laden with some of the children's files. "It was completely out of my hands. The children chose them."

"I didn't even know we had this many different colors of paper."

"Then you haven't gone down on your hands and knees to investigate the back of the crafts cupboard in a while."

He grunted. Fair enough.

"And do you think your little project is working?" He winced at his own choice of words. He'd already seen the fruits of her labor. He shouldn't have patronized her.

"Yes," she answered solidly, refusing to take the bait. "I do think my 'little project' is working. Staff rotas shouldn't be a secret. You're the people the children count on."

He noted she didn't include herself among the staff. Never mind the fact she was endearing herself left, right and center to every living being at the casita. Didn't it matter to her that she would be leaving them? That she was weaving herself into all their hearts and then would just fly back to England without a second thought? That she was leaving him?

It was precisely why he was the way he was.

Pragmatically distant. Nothing was permanent. Nothing lasted forever. Not even family.

"The children have always known there will be *someone* around. Why does seeing who it will be make any difference?"

"Seriously?"

"Yes, seriously." This particular brainchild of hers eluded him. "It's not like we're withholding the information to be all-powerful."

"Then why are you withholding it?" She dropped the files onto his desk, her eyes meeting his for the first time.

"I'm not!" *Okay. That was defensive.*

"Children like to know what's going on around them. They liked to be prepared for things. The same way adults do." She laughed, her blue eyes coming alight. "Except for maybe my sister. And my parents, when they were alive. My mother didn't even like to have a calendar in the house!"

"Is that where you get it from?"

"What?"

"The need to know. The need to plan."

She considered his questions awhile before answering. "I suppose so. To an extent. But my family was exceptionally mad. Musician father.

Artist mother. My sister got all the arty genes."
She smiled, almost apologetically. "Being the
sensible one was what I was good at. 'Oh, thank
heavens we have Harriet to keep us tethered to
planet earth,' they'd say."

A hint of sadness crept into her eyes. Had she
felt it too? The urge to be a free spirit? Only
to take on the role of the dependable one because her family had pigeonholed her into it?
He knew that feeling from his own childhood.
His wild and free sister making the most of her
youth while he'd remained fastidiously tethered
to his books. A fat lot of good being the respon-
sible son had done him. So intent on proving
he was worth something he'd missed what had
been happening before his eyes. He should have
known his sister had needed him. And now time
was punishing him in spades.

"I'll tell you one thing, after seven hours at the
hospital, you're definitely right about needing
your own medical center."

He smiled, grateful for the change of topic.

"You didn't need to fly over from London to
tell me that," Matteo answered drily, instantly
wishing he hadn't fallen back on his "safety net"

tone. "Sorry." He pulled out a chair for her so she could sit alongside him at the long wooden table he used as a desk. "Did I tell you inspections make me touchy?"

"Really?" Harriet feigned disbelief. "That's been *so* tricky to figure out over the past few weeks. I've never met someone who loves showing a girl his spreadsheets so much."

She smirked at him then used her finger to draw a figure eight on one of the desk's bare spots. 'We were waiting over three hours just for X-rays, even with the call you made to your friend. The resident."

"It's a long time for a child to be in pain."

"It's a long time for anyone to be in pain. A and E was teeming. It made me think of the stories of A and E departments in the UK some of my friends from nursing college have told me. A good reminder how lucky we are at St. Nick's."

"How lucky *you* are." *No need to be narky. You're not cross with her, you're cross with the situation.*

"How lucky the *children* are," she countered. "Which is more to the point."

"Well, we do what we can with what we have."

Matteo didn't know if he was apologizing for his country or just being plain old curmudgeonly. Resources were limited. Which was exactly why Harriet was here. To help. He closed his eyes for a moment, took a breath. It was time to stop fighting her so much. Accepting help shouldn't be so…so charged! It was just… For heaven's sake, just look at her! Her pregnancy glow was real, a genuine radiance lighting her up from the inside out. She was one hundred percent beautiful.

"You know what Tico talked about the whole time?" Harriet began to shift the charts into three distinct piles before meeting his gaze. "You."

"*Que?* Whatever for?"

"They love you, these kids. They know how much you do for them. And they want to give back, but…" She hesitated for a moment. "They aren't sure how to show you how much they care."

"What do you mean?"

"You give. You give so much to them, it's easy enough to see. But I don't think it's as easy for you to receive the only thing they have to offer. Affection," she added, unnecessarily.

"I don't think psychoanalyzing me is going to

help us get through these charts," Matteo answered in a way that all but proved her point.

She wasn't the first to have noticed but she was the first brave enough to say anything. But growing up in a house where emotion had been seen as weakness? Where everything had been sheathed in a veneer of false charm? He snapped shut the folder he'd just opened.

"Are you saying I'm not good with the children?"

"No! Not at all." A light flush of pink began to creep along her cheeks. "It's coming out wrong. I'm trying to say they adore you. Absolutely adore you—but they don't seem clear on what it is you want from them."

It could've been a leading question but he could tell it was just Harriet fighting for the children in her own inimitable way.

"I don't want anything from them."

"C'mon. You must have hopes for them. Aspirations. And to get to those, children love to have goals. Have expectations."

"Like your family expected you to keep all the loose ends of their lives together?"

It was a low blow and unkind. She looked away

and he didn't blame her. How could she know she was unwittingly hitting all the points he...?

Oh, Dios. You had to laugh, didn't you?

Harriet was hitting all the points he'd rather gloss over with a veneer of false charm. Push to the side rather than deal with.

He shoved back from his desk, the chair scraping along the floor as he did so and adding to the air of discord.

"These charts can wait. Come with me. I want to show you something."

"Matteo, I need these figures if we're going to present Casita Verde's case to St. Nick's board properly."

He didn't answer.

"Let me guess. This is another one of your 'show naive little Harriet how life really is' lessons."

Matteo pressed his lips together.

Yes. In a way.

"Well, if it pleases his lordship, I'd rather just get on with this work, thanks." She stood to give him a curtsey then looked him directly in the eye. "Just for the record, I think the one here who isn't facing up to how things are is standing right in front of me."

"Very possibly."

He ground his teeth together, eyes linked with hers. She wanted to psychoanalyze him? See why he ticked the way he did? Fine. She'd be leaving in a few days anyway so why keep things hidden any more? "There's an easy enough way to find out why I am the way I am." He opened the door to the courtyard. "Come with me."

"Okay." She nodded. "I will if you do something for me first."

"What's that?"

"Give me a scan."

"Is something wrong?" His chest constricted. To have a baby he was terrified to acknowledge was one thing. To have and to lose that same child? He'd been through that once as an uncle. He didn't think he could survive it again. Especially as a father.

"I'm fine. I've had a bit of spotting since my run-in with Tico, but I'm sure everything is fine. More to the point, if you want me to learn one of your 'life stinks' lessons, then it's only fair we both see what I'm going through. What makes me think life is *amazing*." Her eyes dared him to deny her request.

Matteo felt like a cornered beast. Logic told him Harriet wasn't questioning his good intentions, but all his sensibilities were being overridden with suffocating waves of frustration and anger.

He faced facts every day. He knew she was pregnant and it had been her decision to deal with it on her own. His teeth pressed together so tightly his jaw ached. But he hadn't really given her much choice, had he? Hadn't opened his heart to all she had to offer. But she was questioning the way he *survived*.

Did he wish he could wake up every morning like so many people did and close their eyes to the world's problems? It would make life so much easier. He wouldn't have to scrimp and divvy out help in the way their limited resources demanded. He wouldn't have to turn away those in need to hospitals already sagging beneath the weight of their own overstretched budgets.

Did he wish he could just glide through life as if all the bad things in the world weren't happening around them? His shoulders lifted as thoughts fought for precedence.

No. Of course he didn't. He wouldn't be doing

what he did if he believed that. But something in him knew what he did was still fueled by fury, rage at his sister's unnecessary death. How could he fully open himself up to love—to a future that included Harriet—if what kept him going every day was a ferocious grief at something he could never change?

He took her hand and without a backward glance set off across the courtyard. If she wanted a scan, she could have a scan. And then he'd show her why he had to stay adamantly, *vigilantly* the way he was.

Harriet stood as Matteo flicked on a series of switches. He had a face like thunder but something in her told her they were finally getting somewhere, hitting a breaking point in that cool veneer of his.

She pushed herself up onto the exam table after gulping down a couple of glasses of water, not saying a word as Matteo squirted an excess of lubricant onto the ultrasound wand. She didn't know what had possessed her to make him do this. She could have done it herself, but something in her worried Matteo was denying himself the joy of fatherhood as some form of punishment. She wished she knew what compelled him to live in such a closed-off way when he clearly had a heart of gold. Perhaps the reason was what he was about to show her. And she had to admit she was frightened to know the truth. If he genuinely did not see himself loving someone, having children…

"It'll feel a bit cold."

He was using his doctor voice. The reserved one.

She hitched up her shirt and undid the side zip of her skirt, feeling foolishly embarrassed at having to bare her midriff to him. It wasn't like he hadn't seen everything before! Or touched it. Caressed her luxuriously as if she were a cherished possession. She squelched down the thought and faced the screen as Matteo ran the wand over her womb. She'd be about nine weeks now, by her count. Enough time to see the heartbeat. Her breath caught in her throat and she twisted her fingers into good luck charms. *Please, please, please, let everything be all right.*

She'd seen hundreds, if not thousands of scans herself and yet watching the matrix of gray and black lines comprising her muscles, vessels and internal organs take shape, revealing to her what was happening inside her body was suddenly overwhelming. She kept her hands cemented beneath her thighs, knowing that if she didn't, her fingers would want to weave themselves through Matteo's as they saw, for the first time, the miracle they'd created.

"I'm just looking for the amniotic sac..." Matteo paused as he shifted the wand this way and that before holding it steady, his voice softening. "Here's the heartbeat— Oh! Do you see that?"

She nodded, too overawed to speak.

"Twins." He spoke the word she hadn't been able to. "Just like your sister."

And I'll be raising them on my own...just like my sister.

They sat for a moment, each of them absorbing the news, the only sound audible in the small exam room two tiny heartbeats. Harriet watched silently as Matteo gently began pointing out their arms, the two tiny hearts, four little legs and then abruptly he stopped.

"All right!" He made swift work of cleaning up the scanning equipment and officiously tipped his head towards the door. "Ready?"

He was out the door before Harriet had had a chance to wipe the gel off her stomach, register the news she'd just received. Twins!

I'm having twins.

Her heart ached at Matteo's response. What should have been an ecstatic moment between parents had been clinical and cursory. And yet there had been *something* there. A slight choke in his voice, a sheen on those beautiful green eyes of his. There had! Hadn't there?

She refused to let herself cry, knowing she was the only one to blame for the scenario. If she hadn't insisted he do the scan… Oh! Who was she kidding? She still would've wondered what his reaction would have been. Would've ached to know how he responded to the first sight of his own child—*children*! Well. Now she did. She tugged down her shirt, secured the fastener on her skirt and yanked open the clinic door, uncaring that it shut with a reverberant slam.

"Where are we going?" Harriet raced alongside Matteo, needing two or three steps to each of his single strides as he bashed out a text on his phone with his free hand. He should slow down. He should be compassionate. Hold her hand, swing an arm around her shoulder, pull her into his arms and kiss her with all of the love he held for her, but if he stopped now everything he'd worked towards would disintegrate.

He needed her to see. Needed her to understand why he couldn't open his heart to those two perfectly formed children they had created. Why he couldn't open his heart to her. There was only one place where she would be able to put together all the places. One place where the door to his heart had learned to stay solidly closed.

"Where are we going?" she repeated.

"My parents'."

"You grew up here?"

Harriet thought of the modest two-up, two-down she and her sister had inherited from their parents. It was bigger than most nurses in central London could afford but it was no mansion. Three sets of twins would crowd the place out… but here? There was room for ten sets of twins! Maybe more.

If Harriet had thought the exterior of Casita Verde was impressive, she was entirely unprepared for the splendor of Matteo's family home.

She had a cloudy memory of him mentioning private jets but had chalked it up to Latin machismo. Oops.

The Torres family home could easily be mistaken for a boutique hotel or the embassy of one of the world's richest countries. The towering edifice was composed of beautifully hewn stone, painted a brilliant white. A whiteness presently taking on the hues of the setting sun. A few steps led up to an impressive portico flanked by two intricately crafted wrought-iron gates. Matteo ascended the steps in seconds as if his body had memorized the fastest route in. Harriet had no doubt he could do it blindfolded.

"Why exactly are we here?"

"For supper." He smiled at her with a charm she suddenly understood only a man who had grown up among so much privilege could perfect. Quite a shift from the stony-faced mute man who she'd given silent speeches to throughout the deathly quiet taxi drive.

How on earth she could have fallen in love with someone so prone to stormy moods was…

The thought shivered through her as she reached his side.

Love. Yup! That old chestnut was still setting off light displays in her heart! Annoyingly. This whole scenario would be about a thousand million times easier if she just…didn't…care. Or enjoy staring at his backside so much.

As she ascended each step she realized it wasn't just the pregnancy that had changed her life. It was her love for Matteo—as frustratingly one-sided as it was. From the moment she'd arrived in Buenos Aires she had really *lived*. And it had changed her. She'd been seeing new things, learning new things, thriving in an environment that wasn't dependent upon her—one she hadn't been obliged to feel needed in. It felt like gaining access to a whole new world she hadn't realized existed before.

She glanced across at Matteo, who was pushing open the broad front door without knocking. She was grateful for the gift, the gift of confidence. The door opened into an impressive foyer—and that confidence all but slithered away. It was like entering a different world, one miles away from the hectic hustle and bustle of the massive city, from the mayhem of the casita. A uniformed housekeeper was rushing to the door as Matteo pushed it open. He smiled broadly, kissed her cheeks and held the gray-haired woman at arm's length, hands on her shoulders as he asked a handful of questions, his voice warm with affection.

He introduced them quickly, efficiently before indicating to Harriet that she should follow him into an intricately tiled inner courtyard. Was this man the real Matteo? A man who looked perfectly at home among expensive antiques, servants, comfort? A life without even a hint of the despair they saw on a daily basis? Or was the Matteo at the casita the real one? The one who didn't mind getting grubby? The one who stayed up all hours to get a much-needed grant for funding?

"Mama! Como esta?"

Matteo's arms opened as a beautiful woman, perhaps in her sixties, approached. She was immaculately dressed—heels, sleek trousers, a silk blouse that seemed to have never encountered a wrinkle or the bloom of perspiration that Harriet was experiencing.

Harriet suddenly felt uncomfortable in her "uniform" of A-line skirt and flowery cotton blouse. She nervously ran her fingers through hair she knew could've done with a bit of primping. An untidy contrast to her hostess's jet-black hair pulled smoothly back into an immaculate chignon. Glints of light caught the pair of discreet diamond earrings she wore. A green pashmina, shifting across her shoulder line, brought out the same verdant sea color as Matteo's eyes. At least she knew where he'd got his eyes.

It was difficult to tell if the effusive greeting was a happy ritual or a practiced nicety. Was this what Matteo wanted her to see? A man in control of each microscopic moment?

"Harriet." Matteo beckoned her to join them. "Come, I would like you to meet my mother, Valentina Torres."

As his mother turned to her, Harriet could see her expression shift. Whether it was good or bad eluded her. She felt like shrinking behind one of the enormous pot plants before suddenly remembering…this woman was going to be a grandmother to her twins! She put on a smile and stepped forward.

"So lovely to meet you," Mrs. Torres murmured into her ear as they exchanged air kisses and a variation on an embrace. The greeting was, Harriet realized, terribly... *English*.

The rest of the evening passed in a blur. Matteo's father—Franco Torres—appeared a few moments later, incredibly handsome, terribly charming, straightening his cuff-linked cuffs before offering another series of air kisses. A manservant with a drinks trolley followed in his wake. Harriet was unable to refuse the gin and tonic they insisted all British people wanted but discreetly tipped it into one of the enormous tree planters after a discreet nod of the head from Matteo. It was strange but the move made her feel they were complicit, as though they were finally sharing her pregnancy together. It was a feeling she knew she probably shouldn't get used to, but she liked it. More than was good for her.

She saw Matteo whispering to the servant, who traded out her empty glass for a soda water with lime, complete with a knowing wink. Could he tell? Or had Matteo forewarned him? Unlikely... Her eyes met his, but under the scrutinizing gaze of his parents they were impossible to read.

As the evening got underway, it was a relief to discover Matteo's parents...her babies' only grandparents…were utterly charming. Incredibly well traveled, well read, full of *bon mots*. The evening, conducted mostly in English for Harriet's sake, was nothing less than delightful. And immaculately polite. Harriet was reminded of England's gentry and the slavish obedience to manners above all else. Decorum over honesty? How would they take the news that their son had knocked someone up and wasn't exactly seeing the rosy side of fatherhood?

Then again…what was it exactly Matteo wanted her to see? That his parents were rich and lived by the Miss Manners rulebook? There was something else there. Something deeper, and her heart went out to him. It was clear he and his parents lived very different lives. But there was only so far the apple could fall from the tree. After all, she was who she was because of her family.

Their eyes met as one of the maids began clearing the table and another brought a bowl of fresh fruit along with some delicate pieces of cheese topped with something she'd never seen before. It didn't matter. She wasn't really hungry. Sitting across from the man she loved when loving him would be impossible seemed to blunt her senses.

What was he telling her by bringing her here? What were his eyes saying? She sought answers in their green depths, the tug of connection so strong it almost felt physical.

"Harriet? Have you tried *queso y dulce*?" asked Matteo's father. "This is quince jam together with a sharp cheese. I think you have it in Portugal. You must know it, yes?"

She dragged her eyes away from Matteo's, feeling as if a conversation they'd been having had been abruptly interrupted.

"I—I'm sorry?" She shook her head and registered his father's words. "No. I've not traveled much."

"Has Matteo not shown you the hospitality of the Porteños?" His mother scolded her son in advance of his response.

Harriet shook her head, then said, "We've been to the zoo!"

Again, their eyes met. *What was he trying to say?*

"The city has so much more to offer than the zoo." Mrs. Torres trilled a short musical laugh. "Surely, *amorcita*, Matteo has let you out of your…" she looked up towards the lavish chandelier illuminating the dining table as if it would help her find the best word "…place of work to enjoy some of the nicer sides of our country?"

"You mean Casita Verde?"

Was that a shudder? Had his mother just *shuddered* at a mention of the incredible place her son had built from scratch?

She caught Matteo's eye again. This time his expression was perfectly clear. It said, *See? This is where I come from.*

"You're absolutely right, Mother. I *have* been remiss. Perhaps I should start now," Matteo said brightly, rising from the table and nodding in turn to each of his parents. "Our visit was unexpected and you no doubt have plans for the evening. You wouldn't mind if we missed out on coffee in lieu of a bit of a tour. Would you?" he added, as if they had a choice. He'd already circled the table and was pulling out Harriet's chair so she, too, could rise.

"Of course." His mother silently clapped her hands together, her forehead relaxing a bit as if the evening had, after all, been more taxing than she'd let on.

"It would be a shame for Harriet to miss out on the true delights of Buenos Aires. Why don't you take her to the plaza?"

"Plaza Dorrego?" Matteo's silver-haired father joined in with a glance to his watch. "Splendid idea. There won't be too many tourists this time of year. Yes!" He clapped a hand on his son's shoulder and spoke as if it had been his idea all along. "Take Harriet for a dance in the plaza. A splendid idea. Would you like one of the cars?"

"No, thank you, Papa. We can walk."

Harriet had to press her lips together to suppress a smile at his parents' collective horror at Matteo's suggestion of walking. She jumped in to second his idea.

"Walking would be lovely. Especially after such a delicious meal."

"But you hardly touched a thing!" his mother protested.

"I did! I really enjoyed it!" Harriet insisted, suddenly doubting her own words. The maids had been so deft in shifting away plate after plate she hadn't really noticed if she had nibbled or devoured the four-course meal.

"Shall we?" Matteo reached out a hand to her.

Warmth and comfort immediately worked their way through her as they touched. And she was grateful for it. Her mind was spinning from the evening. Maybe now he would explain what this had been all about. So he was rich. Or at least his parents were. And they behaved a bit like characters in a costume drama. Did that make him a bad person? Hardly!

They bade a hasty farewell and as they went out into the cooling evening air Harriet felt as though she was drawing her first true breath of the evening.

"They do that," Matteo said, his eyes straight ahead, his warm hand still enveloping hers as they walked away from the city mansion.

"What?"

"Impose their world over the real one. I sometimes find it hard to breathe in there. You did well."

Harriet nodded, hoping he would continue.

"Did you notice everything they *didn't* talk about?"

"What do you mean?"

"What did they do when you mentioned Casita Verde?" He glanced at her before picking up the pace. It was clearly going to be a brisk walk to the plaza.

"I don't really recall." Saying she'd seen them shudder wasn't really what she thought he wanted to hear.

"That's because they didn't say anything. They never do. Idle chit-chat—it's all they can handle."

"Why?"

"Because if we were talk about us…our lives, what I do and why I do it…it would be acknowledging their biggest mistake."

Harriet was nearly jogging now, his pace was so fast.

"Sorry. Please, Matteo. My legs aren't as long as yours." She released his hand, needing to steady her pace. Too much was whirling round her mind to make sense of things.

"Lo siento, amorcita." Matteo stopped, steepling his hands and pressing his fingertips to his lips. "I always get heated when I see them. I apologize. Here." He took her hand again and turned her towards a small cobbled side street lit with string after string of lights bulbs twinkling over a scattering of outdoor tables and chairs. His hand slipped to the small of her back as they worked

their way through couples and groups, all finding just the right place to sit and enjoy the balmy evening.

"Let's get a drink and I will tell you what I should have told you when we first met."

Harriet felt her heart lurch to her throat. So much for breathing more easily!

Matteo laughed softly when he looked at her expression. "Don't be scared. It's nothing to—" He stopped himself, his smile shifted into a tightening of his jaw. Whatever he'd been about to say was no laughing matter. "It will explain a lot."

CHAPTER TEN

MATTEO GUIDED HARRIET to a quiet table away from the pedestrian traffic but close enough to the edge of the outdoor seating area to see the plaza spreading out before them. He could see the dazzle of lights reflected in Harriet's eyes, her hips and shoulders shifting intuitively to the tango music that almost always played deeper within the plaza's depths. How to begin?

He bought himself a few more precious seconds of thinking time by calling over the waiter and ordering a glass of Malbec from the Patagonia region for himself and a sparkling water for Harriet, knowing she would refuse an offer to join him with wine.

"You're not going to tell me you murdered someone, are you?" Harriet giggled nervously, her paper serviette quickly being reduced to shreds between her fingers.

"No." Matteo looked her in the eye. "But I am going to tell you about the death of my sister."

Harriet's hands flew to her mouth, her eyes wide with horror.

"I didn't know you had a sister! Oh, Matteo…" She instinctively reached out a hand to touch one of his. "I am so sorry."

"You weren't to know." He looked up, thanked the waiter for their drinks—waiting until he'd set them on the table and left before continuing. This story wasn't just difficult to hear. It was almost impossible to tell.

He drew lines in the condensation forming on the table alongside Harriet's bottle of chilled water as he spoke. "It was a long time ago. Well, when I was nineteen and Ramona was sixteen— so just over fourteen years. Fifteen?"

Harriet gave a small shrug. How would she know? It was his story to tell and it would be easiest if he just got on with it. He sucked in a breath and continued.

"My sister fell pregnant at sixteen and, as you can imagine now that you've met my parents, the news wasn't something they would be thrilled about. The teenage daughter of Franco and Valentina Torres pregnant? The scandal it would've caused." He tutted away the thought. "Rather than risk getting cut out of what you can imagine was a pretty substantial will by telling them, Ramona decided to hide it from us. At least, that's what I am guessing happened—because she left her big brother out of the loop as well." And it still hurt. Until the day he died it would hurt he hadn't been there to help her. If only she had trusted him!

Harriet's eyes remained wide. Free of judgment. Just a clear blue experiencing the pain he was reliving as the words tumbled out.

"I don't know what she was thinking. Maybe she thought she could pay someone to raise it. Maybe she thought she'd find parents to adopt. I don't know. She was too young to go off to Europe without our parents funding it. She never spoke to me or any of her friends. No one." He took a deep draught of his wine before continuing. "Anyway, she was at boarding school, like I had been, so hiding things from our family wasn't too difficult. School holidays? She'd be out with friends. Or so she said. Long story short, she was hiding her changing body from us. All of us. My parents put her prolonged absences down to her going through a wild spell. One she'd grow out of if they just pretended it wasn't happening and I—" He stopped.

This part was on him. He had been at university, doing groundwork courses to become a doctor, for heaven's sake, and hadn't noticed any changes in her. Sure, their paths had rarely crossed but he'd seen her more frequently than their parents had. And he hadn't noticed a thing. She was his kid sister! Maybe a little plump— but what did that matter? She was his kid sister. He loved her. Love handles and all.

"Were you at uni?" Harriet put two and two together without his help.

"Yes."

"It's an incredibly busy time, university. Especially if you are staying on campus."

He cursed under his breath. "You are kind, but you don't have to make excuses for me."

Harriet wanted to console him, but had second thoughts. She could see he needed to get it out. Purge the story that had been holding him hostage all these years.

He took a deep breath, sighing it out before

bringing the tale to its painful conclusion. "She became pre-eclampsic. Hadn't bothered getting seen. Hadn't bothered going to a private hospital for check-ups, though, God knows, she had enough 'pocket money'. Even if she'd had no money, the public hospitals are required to see you if you can't afford treatment. But she was obviously trying to protect my parents from being caught in a pregnancy scandal. Social decorum over saving a life! It sickens me to think about it."

Harriet's fingers had crept back up, pressing the color out of her lips, her eyes just visible above her fingertips. A bit of fringe hung across one of her blue eyes. Instinct had him leaning forward to tuck it out the way before he could think better of it. Her fingers dropped away, leaving just a few centimeters between them. Their breaths, just for a moment, wove together before he abruptly pulled back and took another long draught of wine.

"So did you see her?" Harriet asked.

"Before she and the baby died? No." He shook his head slowly, his mood shifting from charged to contemplative. "No. She was taken to a morgue by someone. We never found out who. And my parents paid off the staff at the mortuary to keep it quiet."

"I can't imagine how awful it must have been." For Matteo. For his parents. Just—collectively awful. Harriet could hardly breathe.

"Losing Ramona was hard enough. It was how my parents dealt with it that made grieving worse."

"Which was?"

"To pretend they'd never had a daughter."

Dry-eyed, Matteo took on the polite persona of his parents, speaking as if he'd been explaining how to change a fuse or mentioning there might be some rain later. "Servants cleared her room. I have no idea where any of her things have gone. People had heard she'd died but that my parents weren't receiving condolences. Or if they sent them staff were instructed to burn anything before my parents could see the messages. It was worse than her being dead. It was as if she'd never existed at all."

"And is the reason you set up Casita Verde."

He nodded. "It doesn't solve many pregnant teens' problems, but at least we help some girls. Some children."

"From what I've seen, you've helped hundreds, maybe even thousands over the years! Not to mention the families who get to adopt those beautiful babies who will be loved and cherished."

"I don't know." Matteo finished his wine and signaled for the check. "Sometimes it's hard to see the point when you know there will never be an end to it."

"But surely you know how much better things are for the girls because of you?"

"I don't know about that. Perhaps." His eyes locked with hers. "Sometimes I feel like it is eating me alive to give them their lives back."

Harriet's breathing caught in her throat. This was it. Whatever he was about to say was at the heart of Matteo's grief.

"In order to do this—to keep the casita alive—I have to set limitations on my own life. I keep myself at arm's length from everything…everyone." He avoided her eyes as he continued. "No girlfriends, no family—absolutely no children. I need the perspective. I need not to care, because if I cared…how could I continue?" He choked out the words, his voice ragged with emotion.

"I hate to point out the obvious, but you don't

really seem as if you don't care. What's the point in it all if it makes you so miserable?" Harriet looked mystified.

Because I've met you.

It's what he should have said but didn't. He couldn't lumber her with such a weight of misery. He gave a wry *humph* and when her expression told him it wasn't enough to justify turning his back on the woman he loved and their unborn children, he continued. "It's ridiculous, isn't it? The unhappy do-gooder. But without my work I can never make it up to my sister. And *with* my work I keep reliving her senseless death again and again. I just keep hoping it will…the happiness of what we do there…I hope it will just happen one day. That one day I will be able to do my work with *joy* in my heart."

Tears leapt to Harriet's eyes as he fought the sting of emotion in his own.

"Do you not see it? All the good you do?"

"The bad statistics will always outweigh the good."

"And that's how you measure your worth? By the statistics?"

"No. It's not that." *I should've been there for her!*

"What is it, then?" she pressed.

"How can I take pleasure in something I wasn't able to fix?"

"You can't," Harriet conceded. "You won't ever be able to. But shouldn't your life be about the future—not about the past? Don't you take any joy from what you do now?"

"Sometimes. Rarely." Matteo shook away both answers, knowing they weren't quite right. He looked her directly in the eye. "When I'm with you."

The silence between them grew as thick as the air. Strangely concentrated for the time of year— as if a tropical storm were brewing. Almost palpable, heated.

Why couldn't he just say it?

Te quiero. I love you.

Anything else would just be hot air. Useless. But when he had nothing to offer her? No future as a family? What was the point?

He became aware of the music floating from the center of the square. He'd done enough talking for the night and knew what he needed now. What he wanted. To hold Harriet in his arms and just be, letting the story he'd just told her shift away into the ether to settle how it would.

"Care for a dance?"

"Oh…" A nervous laugh underlay her hesitation. "I'm afraid I've got two left feet."

"I doubt that." He rose, holding out a hand to her. This could be the last time he would hold her in his arms. He hardly deserved it, but he wanted it—wanted her—so very much. "Come, *mi cariño*. Will you dance with me?"

Harriet slipped her hand into Matteo's, instantly feeling their connection deepen. She had believed her heart could not have felt more open to Matteo than in those moments when he had laid himself bare, had shown her everything that made him the man he was.

She pressed her fingertips into the back of his hand, hoping he knew she was accepting his invitation to take him as he was—a man struggling with the weight of grief. A man struggling to right a great wrong, unable to believe the good things in life were meant for him as well. A man who would live in her heart until the very end of time.

Her hand felt tiny in his. Protected. And yet, as she looked up to receive his gentle smile and an unexpected kiss on the forehead, she knew what she was feeling was true. She'd be able to tell their children their father was a good man. It didn't make the pain of knowing they couldn't be together any easier to bear…but his grief seemed too deeply entrenched for any external power to change. It would have to come from within and, from what she could see, something utterly earth changing would have to happen to him to change how he lived his life. She smiled back, enjoyed the kaleidoscope of green within his eyes, hoping to memorize every detail she could for their children. Her smile turned bitter-sweet as the idea struck that the twins might get those magical eyes and she could have a glimpse of the man who'd won her heart every day.

People and shops, tables and glasses all took on the blur of a film as Matteo pulled her into his arms, slipping the pair of them among the two dozen or so slow-dancing couples. His every touch brought new life to her body. Life she hadn't let herself believe she'd been aching for since they had been together in London. His fingers spread wide across the small of her back as he gathered her hand up with his other hand, holding it close against his chest.

They swayed in time with the music, its cadence adding an additional layer of sensuality to the dance.

She felt his voice vibrating in his chest before she registered the words.

"I'm so sorry."

"Me too." Her whisper was so soft she wasn't even sure if he'd heard her. It didn't matter. What did matter was the here and now. She pressed her cheek against the soft fabric of his dark blue shirt, willing herself to memorize his scent. As if she would ever forget it. Life had made sure of that. Matteo had made sure of that.

The musicians eventually packed up their instruments. Harriet's chest tightened when Matteo finally released his close hold on her, forcing her to acknowledge the moment was over. Their walk home was lingering and silent, each of them at pains to keep the fragile bubble of intimacy they were sharing intact.

Outside the doors of Casita Verde Matteo pulled Harriet to him and kissed her with the slow, heated sorrow of a farewell. Her entire being ached to be with him. Body, heart and soul. It was almost painful—the ache to understand why they couldn't be together. Why they didn't deserve what so many people enjoyed—a simple family life—knowing, at the same time that things were never that simple. Wrong place. Wrong time. Wrong woman?

She tried to shove the thought down. The pre-Buenos Aires Harriet would've thought that. Would have let insecurity overwhelm her. She couldn't let herself drown in doubt again. Not with two babies to care for.

Matteo held her face between his hands, looking into her eyes as if he were trying to see her soul.

"*Te quiero*, Harriet. I hope knowing that is enough."

"I love you, too." Harriet choked back the tears stinging at her nose, not even sure she'd spoken aloud. She forced herself to withdraw from Matteo's sweet embrace and ran towards the secure confines of her little room.

There was no point in torturing herself. Or him. She could see in his eyes he spoke the truth. He loved her, but she wasn't enough. Not enough to help him battle his demons. Not enough to see the good in what he did. Not enough to want to share the joy of raising a family together. It boiled down to what she had feared all along— she wasn't enough.

Harriet knew it was cowardly but frankly she was going to have to shore up whatever reserves of courage she had to face the next... Blimey, the rest of her life without *him*. Her dark-haired, green-eyed lover was going to have to be consigned to the past.

So!

She snapped her suitcase shut and took a final scan of the room to make sure she'd left no traces behind. No evidence for Matteo to find, reminding him she had ever been there. No need to weigh him down with more memories he didn't want to have.

She tipped her head back and sucked in a deep breath, trying her best to get her nose to wiggle away a new rush of tears.

What a palaver.

She gave herself a sharp shake. There wasn't

time to feel sorry for herself right now. Thank heavens for time-zone differences and early-morning flights. She hadn't even bothered trying to sleep once she'd reached her room in those pre-dawn hours. Sleep wouldn't have come. There would be plenty of time for that in—oh, maybe about... When was it children headed off to university? She gave herself a *now, now, don't be like that* look at her reflection in the mirror. There'd plenty of time for a nap when she got home. Early. And hid out from everyone for a few days before she put on her brave face and went back to her old life. Her old ways. Routine. Just the way she'd always like things.

Her heart clenched at the thought.

Her little house and regimented life in the UK had all but disappeared from her thoughts in the few magical weeks she'd spent here. She stepped out of her room, giving the courtyard a quick scan, ensuring wouldn't be any awkward Matteo run-Ins. She'd already spoken with the shift nurse. Explained she had to get home. That it was very important. The nurse knew of her sister and the twins so she had let her come to her own conclusions and had accepted the assurances that "Of course you must go" and "Come and see us again soon". She'd nodded, her heart aching with sadness.

She wouldn't be back. This was it. Farewell forever to the place and the people who had changed her for the better. She was different now and would force herself to remember it. She sniffled. Okay, fine. Maybe a bit of pity party could be indulged in first, but by the time she landed back in the UK she was going to be one hundred percent strong. An independent woman. One who may not be enough for Matteo, but one who was going to be more than enough for their babies. So take that, Mr. Latin Perfection on a Stick! You want to see a mama take responsibility? Love and care for her babies?

This mama is going to love and care for her twins like a wildcat! A really wild wildcat. With English manners! *So there.* Her internal speech ended with a bit of a whimper, but she had to believe it was true—because she was going to have to test that theory again and again and again over the coming months and years.

Babies of her own!

She'd barely given herself time to think about

what it would mean for her. Harriet Monticello… a mother!

She was almost surprised to discover a huge smile was peeling her lips apart before she froze at the sound of Matteo's voice. Her head whipped round. He hadn't seen her, had he? Her shoulders sagged with relief as she pinpointed his voice coming from the clinic. It was still early. From the staccato cadence of his speech and the pauses, he must be on the phone.

She lifted up her suitcase, trying to make as little noise as possible, and in a matter of seconds was out on the street where the people of Buenos Aires were preparing to start a brand-new day.

A brand-new day.

In her case? A brand-life was more like it.

She scanned the busy street, separating the commuters from the taxis on the trawl for customers. Ready to help someone start their life afresh.

The chances of filling the Matteo-sized hole in her heart? Zero to nil. Was there a less than nil?

She raised her arm to the swarm of oncoming traffic, willing a taxi to pull up to the curb sooner rather than later.

If she was going to get on with the rest of her life, she was better off doing so without a backward glance at what never could have been.

He had watched her leave.

He'd seen her crossing the courtyard through the louvered shades on the office door and had actually watched her leave.

A bit of self-flagellation wouldn't have gone amiss, Matteo thought, yanking the cord to the shades up but only succeeding in ripping the ruddy thing from the door entirely. At least a bit of physical pain would take the edge off all the thoughts burning through his mind like corrosive acid.

As the woman he loved had walked out of his life, he'd been on the phone. One of the other homes checking on whether they could send a girl over. She was showing signs of pre-eclampsia and if the symptoms worsened, delivery would be the only option. Another crisis. Another uncertain outcome.

He raked a hand through his hair, enjoying the scrape of his nails against his scalp. It felt raw.

Just like he did. More raw than he could ever re-member feeling.

"Of course, send her over," he'd said, hardly able to bear the sound of his own voice. It was the well-practiced tone of calm, amicability. The one he'd learned from his parents.

He laughed. Not a happy laugh by any stretch of the imagination—more like one of those bot-tom-of-the-well numbers. Mirthless. What else could he do? He'd made his own damn bed and it was time to lie in it. It was what he wanted, wasn't it?

To be left alone to stew in the misery of his sis-ter's death for evermore?

He'd let her walk away.

He picked up the phone handset, tossing it from one palm to the other as he made up his mind. If he was going to stew here forever, he may as well make it worth it. He'd efficiently ruined the chances of St. Nick's going into a co-operative with Casita Verde. They'd want to protect Har-riet and they'd be right.

Harriet. His heart all but punched him in the solar plexus from within. He deserved it. Class-A idiot didn't even begin to cover it. He'd just let the kindest, most beautifully loving woman he'd ever come across—pregnant with his *children* no less—walk straight out of his life so he could mourn something he could never fix. Never in a million years put right.

And there it was. The decision he'd made. Not to fall in love. Not to have children. A wife. A family. This was what it looked like. This was how it felt.

He inhaled deeply, easing the breath out over a long, slow count to ten.

Nope.

Time hadn't changed anything. Ten seconds anyway. Still miserable and only one way to fix it.

He punched the numbers into the telephone handset, his jaw setting tightly as he did. This was one telephone call he had never expected to make.

It was nigh on impossible for Harriet to believe how much had changed in just over a month.

Just four short weeks ago she had taken this exact same taxi journey in the opposite direction. Well, exactly the same plus a few add-ons.

The tango music was the same. The really, really bad traffic that would make the journey cost a fortune and probably make her miss the plane was new. Add to that the heartache and the two minuscule babies growing in her belly.

Those things? Those were all brand spanking new. As fresh as a baby's...

Oh... A smile crept onto her lips.

As fresh as a baby's bottom. Times two.

She rolled down the window, getting a much-needed blast of late-morning air.

It hadn't occurred to her for a second not to have them. *The babies.* It almost made her dizzy to think how microscopically small they would be right now, and she felt, in a way that surely must be crazy, as though she already knew them. These teeny babies created with a man she absolutely adored.

Well.

Right now she didn't like him all that much.

No! Even that wasn't true. She loved him. She loved him heart and soul but he'd made it more than clear her love wasn't enough—it would never be enough. Breaking Matteo's protective veneer of grief seemed all but impossible. He'd made up his mind. No children. No Harriet.

Her hand flew to her tummy and gave it a reassuring little rub.

"Don't worry, little ones. I don't know how we're going to do it but I'm going to make sure you know how loved you are. My little good-luck tokens!" She gave her tummy a satisfied pat as the thought of a pot of Argentina's good luck New Year's beans popped into her mind.

"Mi pequeño haba."

"Usted va a tener un bebé? Felicidades!"

Harriet started at the taxi driver's good wishes. Had she been speaking in Spanish? She gave a little laugh. She'd have to remember everything she could so she could speak to her little ones in Spanish as well.

The smile slipped from her face. For what? So her children could be reminded of the father they would very likely never meet?

The gravity of what was happening suddenly hit her. She sank against the pleather seat of the taxi, willing herself to be strong. All she had to do was get on the plane, go back home and… have twins. Easy. Right?

* * *

Matteo looked up from his paperwork with a start. Was that his *father* crossing the courtyard? Franco Torres III in Casita Verde?

This *was* a day of firsts.

He pushed himself away from the desk and in a few long-legged strides was reaching out a hand to his father, pressing cheeks in the customary greeting—something he did by rote. Only this time it felt different. It felt meaningful.

It struck him how much he missed having his father in his life. He was an incredible business-man, a powerful personality and had been his childhood idol. If he had pushed him, really pressed his parents to talk about Ramona's death, would it have made them any closer?

"Shall we?" His father released his hand, indi-cating they go back into Matteo's office.

Typical. Taking charge of a situation.

"I don't even know why you're here, Papa."

"Come—come inside."

"What? Into my own office?" He felt himself bridling. "You've never even been here before and you're already behaving as if you run the place."

"Now, son—"

"Now, son, nothing!" He reeled round, strangely startled to find they were eye to eye. He was a man facing his father. A grown man. He bit back the insults he could have so easily slung. He was a man now.

It was time to behave like one.

"Please." He gestured to a chair opposite his at the desk. "Have a seat. Mate? Coffee?"

"Coffee, of course." His father had always preferred a rich, dark roast to the traditional tea Argentinians couldn't seem to get enough of.

"Con leche?"

It had been a long time since he'd made his father a cup of coffee.

"*Sí.* Some milk would be nice.

Matteo crossed to the far side of his office to a corner reserved for boiling water, making hot drinks for the girls who came to them—needing the length of time it took to drink a cup of tea to begin to process how much their lives would be changing.

It struck him how easily he could deliver news to his father about how each of their lives could be changing if only things were different. Twins—*his twins*—would be coming into the world. His father would be a grandfather, his mother an *abuela*. He wondered how they'd fall into the roles…grandparenting. Making up for mistakes they'd made the first time round? Or more denial?

He picked up the mugs of steaming coffee and placed them on the desk—one in front of his father and the other where he'd cleared away the pile of paperwork he'd have to finish if work on the sorely needed clinic were ever to begin.

"So?" Matteo put on his best idly curious voice. "What brings you to this part of town?"

Just a few minutes later found Matteo staring slack-jawed at his father.

"You want to pay for the entire building?"

"*Sí.*"

"With no strings?" That was deeply unlike his father. Something was up.

"It's better than taking out a loan, no?"

Ah. That's what this was about. The phone call he'd made to the bank.

"Papa… Father. I am a grown man. I can handle the loan."

"What are you going to pay it back with?" The question wasn't accusatory. It was just sensible.

Matteo stopped his shoulders from going into

automatic pilot and shrug. He didn't know. He didn't have a clue. All he knew was that if he was going to survive life without Harriet he was going to have to work his fingers to the bone to forget—forget everything. The love, the laughter, the tears, the *light*. His children he would never know.

"Would it hurt? To take the money from your father?"

"It's not that, Papa. It's— What has brought this on? How did you even know?"

"Son." His father looked him square in the eye. "Most of our family's money is in that bank. They are not going to take a call from my son without me hearing about it."

Matteo shifted in his chair. This was exactly why he had been hoping to get the funding from England. No family. No strings. No feelings to contend with.

"Your mother and I—"

"Mother is part of this, too?" He was sitting up straight now.

"*Sí*. Of course she is." His father looked amazed that it was even up for questioning. "We make all our decisions together."

"So it was both of you who decided to behave as if Ramona had never lived?"

His father blanched. Matteo instantly regretted the harshness of his words, seeing for the first time how much his father had aged in the past ten years. He had been so handsome, so vital when she had died.

Did he really want to relive the hell that had all but rent his family apart? Something in Matteo told him to keep going. He was feeling the need to bring it out in the open now. Feeling it deeply.

"Is that what you think happened? That we just erased her from our minds? Our hearts? Is that what you think of us?"

He didn't need to say yes. He knew his face told his father everything.

His father's shoulders sagged as he accepted the information and the pair of them sat in silence, registering what had just transpired.

"Do you know what your sister said when she came to us?"

Matteo pushed his chair back from the desk. *What?*

"*Que?* She told you?"

"Yes, what did you think? She wouldn't involve us in something so huge? So life changing?"

"I just presumed…" Matteo felt the thunderous weight of a new understanding strike him solidly in the chest.

"What? That she couldn't come to her parents and tell them she was in trouble? That we wouldn't be there for her when she needed us most? Is that what you thought?"

"What else could I think? No one told me anything."

His father's hands scrubbed at his face while he eyed his son. How could people so close have so much hidden away from each other?

"We thought we were doing the right thing."

"By letting me think she died out there because you rejected her?"

"By letting you think it was her choice."

"To die?"

"No, of course not, son. To leave. It was her choice to leave us."

"And that's why you didn't tell me—because you'd been rejected?" Matteo felt his rage dissipating.

"We didn't tell you in part because we didn't

have the words. We'd failed. We'd failed as parents. She didn't want us. Or want our help. And you were so angry. At the world, at us. It wasn't like telling you then would've changed anything."

"So why are you telling me now? Offering this money?"

"The money?" He waved it off as if it were nothing. "We have too much. How could we give it to causes other than the one our son works on, eh?"

"You didn't really seem to think so when I started Casita Verde."

"You didn't want the help. Would've thrown it back in our faces and we were too fragile then. We thought—we thought if we kept our distance then perhaps…" He trailed off, unable to continue for a moment. "We thought if we gave you your space there might come a day when you would be more receptive to us, be able to hear our side of the story."

"What made you think that it was now?"

"Seeing you—the other night—with her."

Matteo didn't have to ask who. He felt the twitch in his jaw as his teeth ground together. If it had taken his father ten years to talk to him about it his sister, he damn well needed more than a couple of minutes to talk about Harriet. About the children he would never know.

"How long have you been in love with her?" His father uncrossed his legs and shifted in his chair, dark eyes gently trained on Matteo.

"It's that obvious?"

"As the hand in front of my face." He held up his palm for good measure.

"And here I was thinking I had it all under control."

"Son, you have never—in your entire life— brought a woman home to us. It meant a lot to your mother and me. And we like her. We'd love for you to bring her by again."

"We're a bit late for that." He all but ground out the words.

"*Que?* She's gone?"

"Back to England." Matteo hated saying the words. Hated the truth in them.

"And you will go for her?"

Matteo smiled, scrubbing at his jaw as he did.

"I think I didn't make a very good impression."

Should he tell him? Tell him he was going to be a grandfather?

"*Mijo*—can I give you a piece of advice?"

"I have a feeling I am going to get it whether or not I want it." He gave his father a wry smile, the warmth of connection turning it into a toothy grin.

"Eh…" His father tipped his head back and forth. "You know your father better than I gave you credit for." He pushed himself forward and locked eyes with his son. The first real moment they had shared in years.

"*Mijo*, when you are in the midst of something so painful you can hardly see straight, you often make bad decisions. We made a bad decision, your mother and I. Hell! We've made lots of them! If there were any advice I could give to you now—which I wish I'd known then, when we agreed to let your sister walk away from us— it is don't be afraid of being wrong. A decision isn't always worth sticking to. Particularly one made in the heat of the moment."

Matteo felt the frenzied wheels of indecision churning in his mind begin to shift gear. Re-group.

What would it mean if he were… He could barely believe he was letting himself think the thoughts. What would it mean if he were to change his stance? God knew, he loved Harriet and when he had found out she was pregnant his first reaction had been a private swell of elation. One he'd hidden from Harriet as they'd each seen, for the first time, two little heartbeats. Chances were high Harriet wouldn't have him now. Not after the way he had treated her.

But...the spark of possibility reignited his heart rate.

"Papa?" He pushed himself up and out of his chair.

His father waved away whatever it was he was going to say.

"Go. We will see you later?"

He gave his father's shoulder a warm squeeze and dropped to kiss his cheek.

"Yes. Come for dinner," his father called out to him, the words following him into the courtyard. "You whet your mother's appetite to see more of her son. And perhaps a daughter-in-law?"

If there is even the tiniest chance, Papa...even the tiniest of chances...

CHAPTER ELEVEN

"CAFÉ CON LECHE, por favor." Harriet enjoyed hearing the Spanish roll off of her tongue, the waiter accepting her order as if she had lived here all her life and having coffee in the square was perfectly normal. She'd missed the early flight and sitting in traffic for the next one when it was ten hours away? *Bleuch.* The world wouldn't mind if she indulged in just an hour or so in the square where she had last been in Matteo's arms.

She started. Things were different now.

"Descafeinado!" she called after the retreating waiter. It would be decaf from now on.

The waiter tipped his chin upwards, acknowledging her change of order. There would be so many changes to come.

She settled back into her chair, trying not to let herself feel too overwhelmed. This was a good idea. *No, it isn't.* Yes. It. Is. She scolded herself. Matteo wasn't evil, he was…he wasn't able to free himself from the past. So she'd let herself indulge in the past for a bit—a past she'd have to let go of if she were to continue with any sort of strength.

Her mind flicked to her sister, busy with new-born twins. A twist of excitement squirmed through her. She would be telling her sister her news soon enough. Pregnant with twins! She gave a panicked little laugh. Wouldn't it be chaos in their little London house? Two sets of twins, two single mothers... She chided herself for not ringing Claudia sooner. Tell her what was happening. Ask her advice. And how would she begin? *Remember that sexy Latin doctor I told you about?*

"Your coffee, *señorita*."

Harriet froze. She knew that voice and it wasn't that of the young waiter who had taken her order. *Had she just conjured Matteo out of the ether?* She didn't even trust herself to turn around. Her eyes barely moved as the cup of coffee was slipped onto the table by a hand she also knew very well. Her eyes worked their way up along his wrist...a bit farther up, the sleeves of a white linen shirt were bunched once or twice over a well-defined forearm, proof the warmth of the day had increased. She smiled at the thought of just how lovely winter was in Buenos Aires. There would be a tiny bit of summer left in Britain before the days began to close in. Before the cold, dark British winter began.

Her vision began to blur as tears filled her eyes.

"What are you doing here?" She spoke more to her cup of coffee than to Matteo. She didn't dare look at him.

"I've come to tell you what a fool I have been."

Harriet turned at his words, the previously un-spilled tears trickling down her cheeks as she did so.

"Come now, *amorcita*." Matteo used the backs of his fingers to brush away her tears, tugging out a fresh handkerchief with his other hand as he did so.

"How did you find me?"

"I—I didn't," he confessed. "Not in the strict-est sense."

A streak of disappointment shot through her. Another mistake.

She tugged her hand away from his.

"No, *mija*. Listen. If I was trying to avoid you—

would I have brought you your coffee? Be sitting here with you?"

Harriet kneaded her lips in and out of her mouth a couple of times, searching his beautiful green eyes for answers. Could she trust in him?

"Why are you here?"

"I wanted..." He hesitated. "I wanted to come back and think about last night. About telling you I loved you but that I couldn't offer you anything."

The words hung between them, heavy with self-recrimination.

Harriet shook her head. What was the point in this? More *Poor me* before she long-hauled it back across the Atlantic? She had enough baggage, thank you very much.

"So you've come here to make me feel worse than I already do? No, thank you." She picked up her handbag and signaled to the waiter for the check. If the wounds she was already treating were going to be made deeper, she would have been better off sitting in the departure lounge all day. At least there she could think clearly about the future.

"No, not at all. *Por favor*, Harriet. Sit down."

Matteo wasn't pleading but there was a depth of emotion in his tone that compelled her to stay put.

She gave him her best *I'm listening* face in a valiant attempt not to crumble to bits all over again.

"I came to try and re-create that moment in my mind, to try and picture how different things would be if I had just stayed open to possibility. *To love.* To love you, to love our children—" His voice broke as he continued. "I don't think I was ever able to see how it would be possible to love a child of my own without feeling I'd betrayed my sister."

"And what makes you think you can now?" Harriet struggled to keep the defensiveness out of her reply.

"You."

Matteo's beautiful green eyes met hers.

"What are you saying?"

"I'm saying you make me better, Harriet Monticello. You helped me see I can be stronger, more courageous and capable of loving. I love you, Harriet. *Te adoro. Eres mi angel!*" He raised his voice as if he were making a joyous proclamation to the square. Which, she realized with a sudden laugh of pure delight, he was.

Her eyes widened, lower lip caught between her teeth. This was a huge about-face. Could she believe him? His expression quickly sobered as the smile dropped from her eyes. "You're my angel, Harriet. The woman who has made me see that life is for living, not regretting. Can you forgive me?"

"What for?" Harriet couldn't even say the words. Her hands did an automatic trip to her midriff, weaving her fingers together across her belly.

"About our babies?"

"Twins can be a handful! Pregnancies don't always go smoothly," Harriet interjected, her eyebrows shooting high above her eyes. "You know what happened to my sister."

"Two babies? Maybe there'll be more after! As many babies as you want." Matteo's eyes glistened with excitement, his own hand reaching out to cover hers so that they lay entwined together on her belly. "There is one thing, though."

"What?" The word shot out of her. She couldn't do this, ride the emotional yo-yo. Not anymore.

"Will you marry me?"

They were words she had never even let herself imagine she would hear from him. She pored over every detail of his face, trying to glean the depth of truth in his intentions.

"Harriet?" Matteo teased her fingers out of the fists she had clenched them into. "Harriet Monticello…" he slipped from his chair and dipped onto one knee "…will you do me the honor of becoming my wife?"

Her nod was so slight at first that Matteo wasn't entirely sure it was a yes. And then it grew, bit by bit until he was certain Harriet had accepted his proposal.

Without a moment's further hesitation Matteo scooped her into his arms to take kiss after long-awaited kiss from her beautiful lips, a handful of nearby coffee drinkers applauding as they did so.

"It was fate, wasn't it," she whispered against his lips as their breathing steadied, forehead pressed to forehead. "Coming to the plaza."

"If fate hadn't lent a hand, *amore*…I can assure you I would have searched and searched the world until we were together again."

"Forever?" she added, knowing in her heart it wasn't necessary.

"Forever a family."

CHAPTER TWELVE

"I CAN'T BELIEVE it's going to be so big!"

"This is what happens when my father gets involved in anything." Matteo's hands made a shape of something regular sized then ballooned them until it was out-of-control enormous.

"You're not basing that on my ridiculously huge stomach, are you?"

"Of course not, my love. Although…" Matteo eyed Harriet's ever-increasing belly with a studied eye, running a hand across it for good measure. "Are you sure there aren't triplets in there?"

"*Oh, Dios!* I hope not. I think two will be quite enough, thank you."

"You wouldn't have three?" Matteo feigned a hurt expression.

"Of course I would, my love." She went up on tiptoe to give him a peck on the lips, staying just long enough to qualify her answer. "Just preferably not all at once. Besides…" she dropped back onto her feet "…it would be nice for Nicolette and Ramonita to have a little brother to tease one day."

"Ever the practical one." Matteo wrapped a protective arm around his wife's shoulders, dropping a kiss atop her honey-blonde head.

"Practical?" Harriet laughed, thinking how much in her life had changed so quickly. After a whirlwind tour in London to meet up with her sister, the twins and her sister's new husband, they'd come back to Argentina. Now—less than a year after hiding behind a curtain at the first sighting of her Argentine hunk—she was living in a new country, opening up the Ramona Torres Memorial Clinic, married to a man whom she couldn't have dreamed up if she'd tried…and with twins on the way!

"If you call this practical, I'm happy to stay that way." Her eyes widened suddenly, a sharp pain taking hold of her belly. "I think, darling—if we are to be practical—you better hurry up and cut the ribbon for the clinic. I might be needing it very, very soon!"

* * * * *

Look out for the next great story in
THE MONTICELLO BABY MIRACLES *duet*

TWIN SURPRISE FOR THE SINGLE DOC
by Susanne Hampton

And if you enjoyed this story, check out these
other great reads from Annie O'Neil

LONDON'S MOST ELIGIBLE DOCTOR
ONE NIGHT...WITH HER BOSS
DOCTOR...TO DUCHESS?
THE FIREFIGHTER TO HEAL HER HEART

All available now!